# LITTLE BLUE MARBLE 2022

# WARMER WORLDS

## EDITED BY KATRINA ARCHER

A Ganache Media Book

Vancouver

"I Hope This Email Does Not Find You" copyright © 2022 S. G. Baker. Originally published in *Little Blue Marble*

"A Sea of Plastic" copyright © 2022 Bo Balder. Originally published in *Little Blue Marble*

"What to Expect When You're Expecting Advanced Life-Forms" copyright © 2022 Jason A. Bartles. Originally published in *Little Blue Marble*

"Unpredictable Weather Patterns" copyright © 2022 Leigh-Anne Burley. Originally published in *Little Blue Marble*

"Cetacean Reprocessors, Inc." copyright © 2022 Jason P. Burnham. Originally published in *Little Blue Marble*

"The Windtech" copyright © 2022 Victoria Brun. Originally published in *Little Blue Marble*

"What I Do to the Earth, I Do to Me" copyright © 2022 John Paul Caponigro. Originally published in *Little Blue Marble*

"Demeter Seeks Persephone in the Year 2210" copyright © 2022 Priya Chand. Originally published in *Little Blue Marble*

"The Fisherwoman" copyright © 2021 Philip Charter. Originally published in *Loft Anthology I*

"Beneath Everything the Future Still Exists" copyright © 2022 Maggie Chirdo. Originally published in *Little Blue Marble*

"Forward Momentum and a Parallel Toss" copyright © 2020 AnaMaria Curtis. Originally published in *Clarkesworld*

"Sea Turtles" copyright © 2022 Monica Joyce Evans. Originally published in *Little Blue Marble*

"The Trials of the *Thorsten Haugen*" copyright © 2022 J. G. Follansbee. Originally published in *Little Blue Marble*

"Speciation for the New Millennium" copyright © 2002 Jon Hansen. Originally published in *Star\*Line #25.6*

"Helianthus" copyright © 2022 Liam Hogan. Originally published in *Little Blue Marble*

"Yard Work" copyright © 2018 Kevin Lauderdale. Originally published in *Poets/Artists, "Chronicles of a Future Foretold,"* Curated by Samuel Peralta

Cover design by Katrina Archer

www.ganachemedia.com

littlebluemarble.ca

# LITTLE BLUE MARBLE 2022

## 2022

### WARMER WORLDS

*For Ukraine*

# CONTENTS

# INTRODUCTION

WELCOME to the collected stories and poems of *Little Blue Marble* from 2022. All of these stories are available for free online because *Little Blue Marble*'s mission is to educate and inspire, not to make a profit. We thank you, however, because your purchase of this anthology will help us bring the world more great stories about the climate crisis, and keep our mission on track.

2022 seemed to be the year that a great many headlines screamed "Climate Change Is Here!" There's no denying the march of severe weather event after severe weather event: Hurricane Ian in Florida, Hurricane Fiona on Canada's Atlantic coast, the dramatic shrinkage of the Colorado River basin, and severe drought in China. As I write this at *Little Blue Marble* Central on Canada's Pacific coast, it is mid-October and there is no sign yet of the start of rainy season, which usually begins in September.

And yet, the headlines feel disingenuous. Climate change has been here for years. The difference now is that more and more people are noticing that "climate change is here for *me*." It was easy to ignore the problem when one could pretend to remain unaffected. As more and more homes are lost to storm surge, as wells and rivers dry up because there are no more glaciers to replenish aquifers, as wildfire smoke makes more cities unliveable during fire season, humanity is having to come to terms with the consequences of its inaction.

A great many climate scientists are expressing alarm that the severity of weather impacts is increasing at an even faster pace than predicted. Poll after poll shows climate change creeping up the list of voter concerns in North America and elsewhere. It can only be hoped that our leaders will stop dithering and start actually leading, so we can minimize the already considerable damage and loss of life.

In Europe, a despot funded by the profits from fossil fuels wages an unprovoked and unjust war against Ukraine, while waving the threat of a frigid winter over the citizenry of Europe. It can only be hoped that this convinces those governments to wean themselves off dirty fuels produced by corrupt regimes.

In the meantime, *Little Blue Marble* offers you a vision of warming worlds, and our sympathies and support to the brave people of Ukraine.

Stay safe out there, good readers.

— *Katrina Archer, Publisher & Editor, third-generation Ukrainian-Canadian,* Little Blue Marble

# MISS ANGELA DEAN

## M. V. Pine

ALABAMA hadn't changed a whole lot since Grandpa's time. Born in 1993, had he lived just a smidge longer, he'd've lived in three centuries. As it was, nineteen-year-old Sam was riding in the backseat of Papa's car boat, watching the murky waves of the swamp lick the boat's anonymous sides as they headed to clean out Grandpa's "estate." It was too grand a word for a house built in what was a 100-year flood path in 2035, but Papa called it an estate on the news so he didn't look bad to voters.

The sea air blew through the cracked windows and over Sam's blond hair, just long enough to be tied back into a ponytail and keep journalists from asking questions. Fortunately, Papa actually let Sam wear pants instead of a skirt today. He claimed this decision was spurred by the muck in the New Marshes; Sam knew Papa didn't want anybody recognizing their governor and his kid out in the sticks.

"I'm just dropping you off, you hear?"

Papa'd said that a dozen times. Sam muttered, "He's dead. Least you could do is apologize to his ghost or something."

"I will turn this boat around."

"Y'ain't even held a conversation with him in ten years —"

The boat slowed in the marsh, drifting past concrete tendrils of flooded relics and the swamp trees that'd taken over.

"Your job is to clean his place out before that woman of his comes through, and nothing else, so help me god." Papa's white, white teeth peered out from his sneer. His tan face— just tan enough to appeal to a specific working class, not too tan to annoy the rich—was carving new canyons into itself.

Sam had a thousand retorts. But he didn't speak. Just held Papa's ideal blue eyes and thought, *One day, you'll notice we ain't talked in ten years either.*

"Shouldn't've fucking named you after him, should've known that'd bring trouble." Papa cursed as he steered the boat forward, around dark splotches in the brown water, and cut through blue algae that spread as far as the eye could see.

When the stern hit the mud, the tires lowered and pulled the boat across the half-liquid shores. Eventually, they got off the back waterways and onto the wet, paved main road. It was old and partially submerged, constructed before municipalities were required to install floating streets, but that was poverty life in the south. They still had foot-deep sewer lines bursting in their lawns out here, too. As Grandpa'd say, if Birmingham didn't have to smell it, it didn't get fixed this century or the next.

They pulled up to Grandpa's blue house just long enough to read the signs staked in the mud—*The Necessary Wars were Unnecessary!*—and drop Sam off before the boat rolled on, Papa not even sparing a glance at the house that built him.

Cinderblocks now raised the house off the muddy lawn. Sam's oversized boots squeezed water out of the dirt with every step toward the front door. Guess he didn't have to worry about tracking mud in anymore.

But he took off his boots all the same. Just because Grandpa was dead didn't mean he wasn't Sam's favourite. After all, Grandpa'd been the only one to call him Sam until Mama gave in last year. He always said the little wins would pile up, always left baggy clothes for Sam in the closet so Sam could get out of the Catholic-school dresses. Cooked all-veggie meals in the cast iron because neither of them gave a damn about posing for the cattle farmers or the dairy industry.

Now Sam stood in his grandpa's kitchen alone, looking for a name or a number for his second flame, the woman he'd started dating after Grandma died ten years ago. Miss Angela Dean. Papa'd never forgiven Grandpa for moving on, even though he'd never looked happier, and never brought his sweetheart around Sam. Maybe no one'd even told her Grandpa was gone.

There were bills on the telecom in her name, mostly hers

actually. The only things addressed to Samuel Stonewall-Jackson were the big, rarely paid things, like the homeowner's insurance, or the medical stuff.

Grandpa'd been sick for a long time.

Sam always knew this was coming, but he'd hoped it'd be decades down the road, even if no one in the New Marsh zip codes tended to live too long. Hoped he'd give Sam a safe place to land a little longer. Craved that freedom only found in Grandpa's presence.

Mama and Papa weren't letting Sam go to college until he stopped "acting up" so much and played his expected role. Went for a pretty social degree. Found a nice man with white, white teeth and a last name that'd won a few battles in the Civil War.

Cleaning out the fridge should've been the least painful thing. But there was no pretending in the food choices, and the ice cream pops Mama wouldn't let Sam eat were in the freezer. Said it'd make Sam round. Sam ate one tenderly, tears welling up as he carried on about the house.

He played the telecom a few times just to hear Grandpa Sam's voicemail, yearning for the day he himself was old enough to be Grandpa Sam, and hoping he had some other accepting family members by then. The world was already too vast, too empty, and simultaneously too oppressively small without Grandpa.

At least Grandpa had found love in the end. Sam didn't remember Grandma as particularly nice or harsh, but the house had blossomed without her. Grandpa's sweetheart had an eye for colourful rugs, and a brilliant closet that took up all but one short rack for Grandpa's clothes. He'd never been a fashion man, the sort to wear a holey shirt until it gave up the ghost, but this lively lady had embroidered gowns in every hue with more sparkles than the night sky in a blackout. She had church hats for days, their wide, flowered brims swaying like the marsh in the first hint of a hurricane, and of course, a purse to match every hat.

Maybe she and Sam could remember Grandpa together. Grandpa's eyes always lit up when he spoke of Miss Angela Dean, or Miss Angela Virginia Hallelujah Dean if he was feeling good. She had to be heartbroken to have lost so deep a love, yet her number wasn't in the contacts or written on any note, and not one of her names popped up on a quick Citizen Search. Well, there was a Miss Angela Dean, but she was twenty-eight and a former Miss Alabama. Sam was fairly sure she wasn't dating his grandpa.

If she was, Papa's anger wouldn't seem *so* awful for once. Ten years ago, Grandpa dating a then-eighteen-year-old beauty queen? Sam would have a couple of questions. But right now, all he questioned was where her toothbrush was, considering the shower was full of what had to be her choice of shampoo.

Papa was going to be back before sundown so they didn't have to drive the swamp at night, but if Sam didn't find her number by then, he'd come back the next day and look. Even if he had to hail a water taxi. He had a couple thousand bucks he'd been saving for uninsured T injections. He could use that to honour Grandpa one last time.

There were two bedside tables, one clearly used more than the other, or more carelessly so, considering the cup rings in the wood. In the marred one's drawers were books, tissues, *sex toys*—

Sam shut that drawer quick.

In the less used bedside table was a single envelope marked *Do Not Toss*.

"Appreciate it, Grandpa," Sam murmured, lips twitching with a sugar-sticky smile.

Maybe he shouldn't crack the envelope's wax seal alone. But it felt like one last conversation to be had, just Grandpa and Sam, and Sam yearned to speak to him one last time. So, he peeled the seal. More paper—some handwritten, some typed—fell out.

Oh god, the typed one was a will.

Sam tossed it on the bed like a curse, like getting it away from him could deny Grandpa needed a will, had died at all. But he had. Miss Angela Dean's number might be in there.

It wasn't. She wasn't mentioned in the damn thing at all. Neither was Papa or Mama, just Sam, Grandpa's name, and an obedient little signature. There wasn't a lot of money, practically none at all, but he'd left the whole damn house to Sam.

Why?

Grandpa knew Sam didn't want to live in Alabama for one more second. Wanted to go up to New York or Seattle or London—

*Sam,*

The handwritten letter addressed him. Somehow knew it'd be Sam that found it. The scrawling, looping cursive was beautiful, almost perfect, and difficult for Sam to read.

*If you're seeing this, I've passed. I'm sorry to have left you so soon. I hope you know, I wanted to stay longer, to meet the bride you chose, and admire the things you accomplished—and you will accomplish so much, don't you think you won't—but the cancer is hitting too hard.*

Already, Sam was crying. Sitting on the bed. Wishing it were all different.

*I worry about you on your own. I worry about you having a roof over your head now that I'm gone, as it seemed like my stability was the only thing keeping your parents from threatening you with homelessness sometimes.*

"It was, Grandpa, it was." Sam choked up, remembering Papa's threats in the garage, and Mama throwing out shapewear, bandages, duct tape, and anything in the house that could be used to flatten breasts down.

*I've never told you this—your parents said they'd never let you see me if I did—but when I was young, I was kicked out for the same reasons. How history repeats itself. It was impossible to get my feet under me while on the streets, and my folks used that to mold me into the man they wanted. I won't let that happen to you. So have my house.*

Sam had to stop. He fled into the bathroom to blow his nose. This opened the world for him. It was easier to pay for college on his own if rent was not an issue. The health insurance people could telecom this address instead of his parents'—

What did Grandpa mean he was kicked out for the same reasons?

Puffy, Sam eased back into the bedroom and trembled as he took up the note.

*I'm glad someone wanted the name Samuel. It's a good name, and you fill it out well. You deserve to live your whole life under the name you want, rather than only your last ten years.*

Oh god.

Sam stared at the walk-in closet of casual and radiant dresses alike.

*I had to write this letter to you because you were the only one I trusted to understand and care. I can't go into that dark night misnamed and misremembered. So, get me a funeral, however small, and promise me this: you'll send me off as the most weed-smoking, wise-cracking, beautiful old lady in all of Alabama: Miss Angela Virginia Hallelujah Dean. Or Angie, if I like you. Remember me this way.*

*As for you: you are so much more than just that politician's trans son. You are strong, you are handsome, and you come from a long history of trans people. Never forget that. Never forget your family is more than your parents.*

*And never forget that I will __always__ be with you.*

*Love,*

*Grandma Angie*

Grandma's signature was as beautiful as her dresses, and her home felt like the warmest hug. Suddenly, the world was wide with hope, and welcoming, and had as much potential as birds must find in the sky.

Sam hugged her note with all his might, "I'll send you off right, Grandma Angie, I will. I promise."

# ABOUT THE AUTHOR

M. V. Pine fixes some of the Pacific Northwest's largest dams. Often, these close calls are the spark of inspiration for a scifi story. When Pine isn't writing or investigating a dam's cracks, they can be found on abandoned logging roads, asking "Where does this lead?" One day they'll end up in a portal fantasy. In the meantime, you can reach them on Twitter: @Madeline_Pine.

# I HOPE THIS EMAIL DOES NOT FIND YOU

## S. G. Baker

DEBRIS crunched beneath Pepper's wheelchair as she rolled along the top floor of the Stonegrove Shopping Mall. Just small scraps, though, the kind she could roll over without her wheels catching. This area of the midsized mall was largely cleared out since most of the community lived up here, where they could access the vegetable gardens on the roof. Up here, folks would sweep up to make Pepper's going easier, but she had to dodge little piles of crumbly ceiling tiles on her way to one of two escalators leading downward.

Natural sunshine shafted in through big overhead skylights. Pepper wore a lemon-yellow T-shirt and orange shorts for this summery day, scrounged from one of the few clothing stores remaining in the mall. The community's scouts had spotted a caravan weaving along the vehicle-choked highway that morning, and she wanted to trade them something useful they could spread to others.

The Stonegrove Shopping Mall had already begun to decline before the slow but inevitable collapse of society—more empty storefronts than full, escalators running for handfuls of visitors, and the elderly using the circular central plaza as climate-controlled walking tracks.

Back then, Pepper had managed the Illumenary Candle Store on the second floor. Back then, she'd used the elevator to get around. Back then, she'd been taking her lunch break in the food court on the fourth floor—a desultory affair of rubbery fries and leathery burger—because she hadn't had time to pack lunch.

Back then, the city power grid, already spotty, had flickered. Surged. Flickered. And failed for the last time.

As the mall had emptied out, everyone had left Pepper behind with a dead elevator. Security guards hadn't even come up to clear out any stragglers because what was the point? The mall didn't matter anymore. It was the end of the world. Everyone knew it.

Up high near one of the broken skylights, a bird trilled. Down below, there came an answering tweet from a man sitting on the bottommost escalator steps where water lapped at the metal stairs. When an upriver dam had sprung a leak, part of the new flow had routed right through the mall's first floor. Everyone had shrugged and cleared a way for it to pass out the other side. Now they had their very own creek, gurgling against columns and around benches.

The man wore khaki shorts and had one brown leg dipped in the water. In his large hand, he held a fishing rod from the old sports outlet. A tall, white plastic bucket sat at his side. Pepper knew it would be filled with fish. Booker was a good fisher.

Moss clung to the rubbery handrail of the escalator that Pepper approached. Previously chugging metal stairs now lay still and silent beneath a plywood ramp laid down its length. A cable pulley system, the very one from the elevator, hung strung along one rail with a big metal tow clip attached to this end. Pepper paused to tie back her dark, curly hair. She then backed up to the clip. With a lot of twisting and stretching, she got the clip hooked to the crossbars beneath her wheelchair. Braided steel nipping at her palms, she let herself down the ramp.

Without power for refrigeration, the food left behind in the food court with Pepper couldn't last long. But at least, trapped on the same level as the food, she could eat. Figuring she would die soon, Pepper had wheeled around the fourth floor, munching gross, cold chicken nuggets, wondering what was happening outside.

Since the power hadn't come back up, she assumed the city had fallen at last, if not the whole country or the whole world. She regretted now that she'd kept working even as the economy slid, but government disability had vanished with any semblance of a government and the remaining corporations were not much given to charity. Still, she would've liked to spend more time crafting artisanal candles of her own before the end.

Her reaction wasn't as blasé as all that. She'd cried a lot.

Lucky for Pepper, as she'd wandered around—aimless, a heavy lump of tears in her chest—she'd found the grill in the burger joint was gas powered. When she'd idly punched the red starter button in passing, blue flames had sprung up underneath the griddle with a *whumpf*, heat licking over her face. Surprised, she'd shut it off at once. But then, with a tiny spark of hope, she'd wheeled every melting bag of ice she could find to the nearest freezer, then dumped all the frozen food in there, too.

She could survive this way, she'd told herself. For a while, anyway. At least until someone found her.

Still, it had taken a long time for anyone to find Pepper. Even then, only because she called.

Pepper had understood the power of light in a dark world. Fortunately, the food court featured a floor-to-ceiling wall of windows, one of the few in the entire mall. Pepper had found cooking oil with the chicken nuggets and shoestrings from a small shoe store and built a crude oil lamp. She'd set the oil lamp on the floor in front of that wall of windows every evening.

*Un*fortunately, the window didn't face the main drag where anyone passing would notice the light, or where she could even see anyone passing. Each night, she'd parked next to the lamp, gazing out into the absolute darkness of an unpowered city for about an hour before blowing out the flame. For all she knew, there was no one out there.

But someone had seen her light.

Sweating, Pepper managed to lower her wheelchair about halfway down the steep escalator ramp before Booker called her name from below.

"Can I help you down?" He stood next to the ramp on the second floor, face tipped up toward her, pointing at his end of the pulley.

Pepper smiled. She loved when people asked first. "Please!"

Booker's added strength made Pepper's trip down much easier. When she got to the bottom, she said, "Thank you so much. Can I do anything for you?" Though their community functioned on trade, it had grown enough that acts of kindness with no expectation of return could flourish again. Still, it was polite to ask.

Smiling, Booker said, "It's my birthday today. Do you have any good jokes?"

Pepper tapped her lips a moment. "What do you get when you goose a ghost?"

"I don't know. What?"

"A handful of sheet."

A snort escaped Booker. He shook his head, smiling bigger. "Yeah, I'd say we're square. Where're you going?"

"My store," said Pepper. "Got 'em to turn the lights on for a minute." Salvaged solar panels had just gone in on the roof, allowing them to save propane for the emergency backup generators now. That meant they could power various areas of the mall for short times if they were careful. "Will you still be here in thirty?"

Booker's expression went a little solemn. "I'll help you when you get back, don't worry. Take your time."

One night, the echo of voices around the mall had woken Pepper. Flashlights had strobed around the central plaza from the first floor as a group of people clattered up the motionless escalator. She'd wheeled out to meet them, holding her hand up against the glare as several flashlights jumped to her in surprise.

"Can you point those somewhere else?" she'd said.

"Sorry!"

Several lights had clicked off and the rest pointed at the floor. Twenty people of varying ages and skin tones had stood clustered together with a middle-aged woman in a business suit at the front. She'd had fake nails, but several were broken off. Her blonde ponytail showed brown roots. Nature taking over. "Were you the one with that light in the window?"

Pepper spread her hands wide, indicating both her wheelchair and her little food-court kingdom. "That's me. Can you help me get down?"

Amanda, as Pepper found out her name later, had exchanged glances with none other than Booker at her side. "Sure," she'd said. "But we wanted to know … can we stay here?"

Pepper had pressed her lips together, fighting back tears. She loved when people asked first. "If I can stay with you," she'd said thickly. She didn't have family in the city to look for her. Nowhere to go if she left. But with a community, she could survive here. "And if you let in anyone with a disability, then sure."

Amanda had directed the group to build ramps around the mall for Pepper and rig up the pulley system. It was no elevator, and Pepper would always miss those, but at least she could get herself around now.

Illumenary still smelled amazing when Pepper wheeled inside. A glorious intermingling of scented candles, incense, wax melts, and bath bombs in lavender, coconut, cotton, rose, citrus, and more. Her original stock, once overflowing the shelves into the clearance bin, had dwindled as she'd brought candles upstairs for light until they'd set up the power generators, then for celebrations and trade. She paused to gather three jars, laying them on her lap. Thick glass clinked as they rolled together.

In Pepper's back office, sunlight poured in over her dusty desk from the single window. Several vines and weeds poked up here and there from piles of plaster and crumbling sheetrock. A young tree had sprouted in one corner, its leaves flicking like big yellow-green coins in a light breeze. This close to the creek a level below, humidity made her keyboard tacky. As Pepper waited for the computer to boot up, she picked up her old mug embossed with the Illumenary logo. Inside, she found a fat, sleeping frog.

Pepper was after a candle-making recipe she'd emailed to herself with an eye to using it for a promotion. It was historical, circulated among candlemakers for the novelty of the crude ingredients. With this, she wouldn't have to worry about running out of candles. She rested her chin in one hand, daydreaming about the spread of the recipe through the caravanners. Passing from person to person until the whole continent could make candles again.

But when she pulled up her inbox, she found an unopened email. It was from her boss up in Cincinnati, dated three years ago, just after Pepper's city had gone dark. The previewed text showed: *I hope this email finds you well.*

Pepper hovered the mouse pointer over the message. Just that wording alone gave her flashbacks to meaningless corporate politeness. So distant and empty and cold.

Three years of unemployment, wherein her value to her community was not determined by her ability to *contribute* but by her existence as a *person*, had made Pepper forget the despair of corporate life. She raised her head from that old computer screen where she had so often stressed about meeting sales quotas and passing district management inspections, taking in the peace of her new home.

She reminded herself she never had to go back.

Pepper clicked the email open. Keys clacked as she typed a response.

I hope this email does not find you.

I hope your office has overgrown with vines.
I hope your chair has collapsed into dust and
that a frog sleeps in your old coffee mug.

I hope you've forgotten about quarterly reports and 8 a.m. business meetings. I hope moths have eaten every single file in your filing cabinet.

And I hope, wherever you are, that it's quiet.

When Pepper hit *send*, a message immediately appeared in her inbox. *Message failed.*

She smiled. No one was there.

Back at the escalator, Booker climbed up from his fishing spot. With the printed candle-making recipe tucked into her pocket, Pepper handed him a candle jar from her lap. A spicy ginger-and-orange scent bloomed between them when he popped the glass lid open for a sniff.

At Booker's delighted sigh, Pepper said, "Happy birthday, my friend."

# ABOUT THE AUTHOR

S.G. Baker is a writer and editor of fiction who penned the *Hopeful Wanderer* web series. She holds a bachelor's degree in English from West Texas A&M University with a focus on writing, editing, and linguistics. Summer has received honorable mention for the 2017 *Writer's Digest* Writing Competition.

Her publications include short stories in *With Words We Weave 2022: Hope* and *Road Kill: Texas Horror by Texas Writers, Vol. 2.* A wanderer and a dreamer herself, Summer travels often to bring the wonders of the world to her stories.

# WHAT'S A PENGUIN?

## S. J. C. Schreiber

MICHAEL stares at the seagull sitting on the ship's railing; the bird, in turn, watches the half-eaten protein bar in the teenager's hand. These pests are everywhere, always on the lookout for an easy meal since most of the fish disappeared. Michael crumbles the plastic wrapper and tosses it at the bird. The seagull takes off just in time and the projectile drops into the sea below, joining the small mounds of trash floating in the waves like miniature icebergs.

He puts his hood up and rubs his hands together, then checks the thermometer on his smart watch: eighteen degrees Celsius. No surprise he's feeling cold; he's never seen the needle go below the twenties before.

His mother appears behind him, wheeling his grandfather in a chair loaded with blankets. Despite his cold fingers and the wind whipping his hair, Michael forces a thin smile. The old man is the whole reason they are on this cruise, a sort of trip down memory lane. It cost them half of their savings, but his mother said it was worth it, because "who knows how long your grandpa will be around." Michael would rather spend the holidays with his friends, diving into virtual reality. They are all only children; population restrictions have been in place for several decades.

"Looking forward to shore leave in a bit, honey?" his mother asks.

Michael shrugs, hands in his pockets.

They had been confined to the luxuries of the cruise ship for the three days since they left port in Denmark. Three days of lavish buffets with exotic treats, the gentle swaying of the boat, and warm air blowing from the vents. He's wary of being surrounded by more water than he has ever seen before, and he can see in the way his mother stares out the windows that she is, too.

It's endless, blue, and quiet.

Nothing like the underground house they live in, safe from the harsh sunlight and unbearable heat. The fire sirens and ambulances rushing through the streets above are a constant backdrop, day and night. They live in what his mother calls "the better part of town," but he's still not allowed to go outside after eight in the evening. And during the day, it is too hot to go to the surface.

"Soon we'll set foot on Greenland," his grandfather says with a nostalgic smile. He seems to be the only one who feels comfortable on the swaying boat. "That's where I met her, you know? Your grandmother. On a cruise just like this one."

Michael stops himself from rolling his eyes. He's heard this story a dozen times, half of them during the last three days alone.

"It wasn't as fancy as it is today. Most evenings we had dried fish and rye bread for dinner."

His grandpa talks about it like it's an everyday occurrence, but Michael has never tasted fish. The few that are being bred in small aquariums for sashimi cost even more than this vacation did.

"One morning, we all heard a loud crack, and went to the front of the ship. The icebreaker had smashed through one of the last remaining ice floes—no one wanted to miss that sight. And that's when I saw her …"

Michael silently mouths the next words.

"… your grandmother. A thick woolen scarf was wrapped around her shoulders and a knit hat pulled down over her forehead, but I knew right away that she was the most beautiful woman I had ever seen."

This next part is new.

"So I walked up to her and asked her if she's excited to see the penguins, knowing full well that there were no penguins in these parts." Grandpa chuckles. "If she would correct me, I knew she was the one. And she did."

The old man falls silent, and his eyes wander over the deep blue horizon, lost in memories. Michael and his mother exchange a glance.

"What's a penguin?" Michael asks.

A tear runs down Grandpa's wrinkled face, but he says no

more. Michael's mother pats the old man's arm.

Less than an hour later, the deckhands moor the gigantic ship to the pier, throwing ropes and barking orders. Michael watches scores of pink flamingos stalk along the shore, picking at the white sand for food. Colourful parrots fly screeching above the boat, and his eyes follow them, until they fall onto her.

The most beautiful girl he has ever seen.

He smiles. Maybe she knows about penguins.

# ABOUT THE AUTHOR

S. J. C. Schreiber (she/her) lives with the elves and trolls (and her cats and horses) in Iceland, the perfect setting to write magical stories where fantasy meets reality. Her work has been published in several online and print outlets and was shortlisted in the Furious Fiction Contest by the Australian Writers' Centre.

# AFTER *STAR TREK:*
# *THE INNER LIGHT*

## Salik Shah

ALL this I saw:
the light you preserved
within after the destruction
of your world,

the slow resurgence
afterwards
in the wandering domes
caressing the new ocean.

Black shadows, artificial suns
—reviving the dry riverbeds
rising from beneath
mycelial networks:

*gaia*
*gayatri*
*sentient*
*earth.*

Once you hammered and poured
—molten skeletons, megastructures.
Shiva's children or a shaman's
dying curse—

I do not know what form
you will take this time
as I radiate and transform
with each mutation.

*We hold onto each other*
*like fresh stitches*
*on old wounds.*
*As we heal,*
*we bond;*
*become*
*untraceable:*
*one.*

In the cold distance a new sun rises.
Know this: you'll survive;
you'll learn to laugh
like a child again.

On abandoned ports, you'll share
hot tea and biscuits,
conspiring in nonstandard Imperial
to save dying worlds:

one wildlife at a time;
one tree, one river,
one coral reef,
one jungle.

Once She held you to her breasts.
Now you carry her
in your bones and flesh
—forgiving, forgiven.

## ABOUT THE AUTHOR

Salik Shah is a writer, filmmaker, and the founding editor
of *Mithila Review*, the journal of international science fiction
and fantasy (2015-). His work has appeared in *Asimov's Science
Fiction, Strange Horizons, Tor.com,* and *The Gollancz Book of South
Asian Science Fiction (Volume 2)*.

# THE FISHERWOMAN

## Philip Charter

THIS is your fourth visit to the botanical biosphere.
Something always draws you back here, even though you
have only one hour of leisure time. You scan your wristband
and enter the glass dome.

The biospheres are teeming with healthy plants and trees.
Mechanical bees flit between the groups of coloured flowers.
Today, you've come to see the rainforest exhibit, but first,
you pass through the Japanese gardens.

An elderly woman sits on a bench overlooking the koi
pond you like. The white and orange fish swim around in
their docile dream, barely causing a ripple. She's been on that
same seat each time you've come here. The chatter of other
visitors filters through the bushes that shelter the pond from
the main pathway.

You clear your throat. "Hello there."

She looks up with kind eyes as if she'd been expecting

someone. "Yes, luvvie?"

"I noticed you often come to look at—"

"The fish? So beautiful," she says. "Blissfully ignorant of what's around them." She coughs into a handkerchief and smiles apologetically.

The woman is right. Those fish exist within the confines of their pool, just as the vast majority of citizens live their entire lives in one place, their movements monitored and controlled. You're one of the lucky ones who can travel.

"It's my medicine, see?" she says, gesturing with her hand. "Three hours every day because of the grey-lung."

One day, it will be you sitting on that bench with a prescription for natural air because of respiratory problems. When you ask if you can join her, she shifts to create more space and pats the seat next to her. You wonder if she remembers anything about life before the Federation and if she was part of the nomadic workforce like you. She's mysteriously familiar. Is her homestory anything like yours?

When you were born, a unique piece of code was added to your identity chip. Everyone has one. It was written by the Scribe, the supercomputer that generates a narrative based on individual DNA. The code is your homestory. Homestories must not be recorded, only told from one person to another, shared when the human connection is strong enough to do so. As you sit, you decide to share yours with the woman in the Japanese gardens. She looks like an older version of you; same broad nose, same thick hair, but she radiates an aura of calm.

"Can I share my story?"

She looks straight ahead at the koi pond and smiles. "Of course."

So many times you've thought of writing your homestory on a folded piece of paper and leaving it by the fish pond, but if it were discovered it would be eradicated. You once found a homestory in an air duct you were upgrading. It was written on the wall in Morse code. Transcribing a few sentences each day was thrilling. It's probably been erased by now.

Others try to tell theirs to everyone they meet, blurting it out and not caring how the other person responds, but it's rare for you to tell your story. You face the woman and begin. "My tale is that of the Fisherwoman, born hundreds of years ago, on an isolated island."

The woman sits up a little straighter. Perhaps she remembers a time when there was land still surrounded by the sea. When the last island was connected via earth bridges built by the bot fleet, the Federation announced it with much fanfare.

"While her husband went in search of new lands," you say, "she would fish the wide ocean inlets and the deeper trenches contained within the brilliant blue reef. Her people called the island the Jewel of Giants, as though her corner of the earth was held together in the turquoise necklace of some greater being."

The old woman sits with her hands on her knees and her head tilted, interrogating each sentence for meaning. The irrigation system nearby sprays out a light mist.

"In her boat," you continue, "she took a net, a flask of water, a hat for when the sun beat strong, and a pail for her catch."

In your world, there are no personal possessions, not even flasks of water.

"Each day she fished in a different place, casting her circular net high and watching it drift down into the sea. While she reeled it in, she hummed the tunes her mother had taught her, loud enough for her to become part of the soundscape, but not so loud she scared away the fish. When her pail was full, she would return to the village."

You've never tasted fish. Animal consumption was outlawed last century. The last wild animals were lost and huge droves of insects now roam the earth. Modern cereals are immune to them, other plants are not. Unfarmable areas are devoted to growing oxygen-producing bushes, designed to poison all pests. The Federation exists in perpetual chemical warfare with its own land.

"And when do the giants come?" the woman asks.

You're surprised she interrupted. "Have you heard it somewhere before?"

"I know it from another perspective," she says.

Your heart swells. If her narrative connects, she might be a blood relative—a great-aunt, or a second cousin. You've never met a relative before, although you spent many nights wondering who they are.

"Sorry," she says. "I'm holding you up."

There may not be time to visit the Amazonian biodome,

but it's more important you deliver the homestory as best you can. You gather yourself and continue. "After many months away, her man returned and together they had a baby girl. She took the child fishing in her canoe, hoping that the songs she hummed would pass down, along with the joy of being a fisherwoman. They lived happily until one day men in bigger boats arrived at their island."

When *you* were a child, you lived underground in an orphanage. Days were routine, with no time allocated to discover or dream. They said you were fortunate to learn a trade and provide a service to the nomadic workforce of the Federation.

Your job in air filtration takes you all over the planet. Over the years, you've seen places you could never have imagined, heard the homestories of countless others—the Warrior Queen, the Great Jewelry Thief, and the Deaf Maestro. But, with so much exposure to unfiltered air, your lungs won't last long.

"These men were giants, their hands callused from rowing across seas," you say.

As if to participate in the story, one of the fish comes up for air and splashes water out of the pool.

"They were bigger than the fisherwoman had ever seen. The men destroyed her village. Roofs burned to black in seconds and the smell of the smoke tarnished the air forever. They killed her husband and took her baby, but before they thrust a spear into her belly, the fisherwoman held up her hand and cried 'Wait!' The men paused. 'I will show you where the fish are,' she said. 'This island has a bountiful supply, but only I know where.'"

You try to imagine what tropical fish looked like. Were they flat and smooth, like the rays in the great botanical gardens of Singapore, or silvery and fast, like the shoals of mackerel in the Nordic Aquarium? You've visited so many public ecosystems, but the Japanese gardens are your favourite. You are drawn to their gentle form, like it's in your DNA. You feel one step closer to the fisherwoman.

The old woman hangs her head, as if sensing further tragedy, but however her story is linked to yours, it can't interrupt the ending of your tale.

"She showed the men her fishing spots and they brought bigger nets from their bigger ships. The nets tore the coral from the sea bed and dragged up sea creatures big and small. While they worked, she hummed the songs she loved, but in her head. The men rejoiced at the size of the larger fish and laughed at the smaller ones. They ate them all until there were none."

The wristband on your arm vibrates, indicating your ticket has five minutes until it expires. You quicken the pace of the story. "After a time, all of the fishing grounds ran dry and the men left in search of new territory. The seas were empty, and nothing would grow in the scorched ground. The remaining villagers lived together, surviving on coconuts and dry roots. This was the fisherwoman's punishment for saving herself."

When you look up, the woman is crying. Large teardrops

run down the tracks of her cheeks and onto the bench.

"Don't cry," you say. "It's only a fable."

She wipes the tears away with a sleeve. Her aura of calm is broken. Her voice shakes as she talks. "I know, luvvie. I know how it ends."

It doesn't matter that your ticket is running out, and that you won't visit the rainforest exhibit. All you want is for the woman next to you to witness the end of the story, and to discover why it affects her so. Were you destined to meet? Orphans can go a whole lifetime without finding the stories that connect to theirs.

In solidarity, you close your eyes and live the fisherwoman's past and future. Her song gets louder and clearer each time. You breathe her air and bear the burden of her decision.

"Wait," the woman says. "Before you finish, I have to show you this." She stands, lifts her right foot onto the seat and rolls up her trouser leg. Etched onto her calf is a small tattoo, its piercing colours contrasting with the metal bench. The image shows a woman in a broad hat, paddling her boat through blue waters. Barely visible at the back of the canoe is a pail.

Your wristband vibrates again but you ignore the warning.

Now you understand what draws you back to the Japanese gardens. A lump builds in the back of your throat. You want to live this moment forever, and cry together with the woman from your homestory.

Before you can finish, she tells it in her own way. "In trying to save herself, the fisherwoman had ensured the death of something more important. For that, she was stricken with guilt." She dabs at her face with a sleeve. "One day, she paddled her canoe far into the ocean until she could not see land. She did not bring a hat, or a pail, or a flask of water." She phrases the words exactly as you would.

The woman starts to hum the beginning to a song but erupts into a coughing fit. Although she must be younger, she has the withered frame of an eighty-year-old.

You remove a tissue and guide her back into the seat. "Relax now. Just rest."

She agrees and you finish the story.

"Visitors to that place maintain that if you hold your ear to the wind on the shores of her island, you can hear the faint humming of the fisherwoman's song."

Each and every time you recount "The Fisherwoman," you leave a part of yourself behind with it. It exhausts you, but builds a desire to hear the story of the person you shared it with. Especially this time. Moving closer, you reach for your biological mother's hand. There is no more time to hear which forces took her away, and how her homestory connects to yours. Not today.

You help her to her feet and embrace the woman you've waited your whole life to meet. You are both part of this place, at one with the koi and the cherry trees of the Japanese gardens. But, she must stay and you must leave. "I'll come back soon," you say. "You can tell me your story next time."

# ABOUT THE AUTHOR

Philip Charter is an English writing coach who works with non-native speakers. Philip's stories have won or placed in competitions such as the Loft Books Short Story Competition, The Oxford Flash Fiction Prize, and the Janus Lit Anthology competition. He is the author of two short-fiction collections and a novella-in-flash, *Fifteen Brief Moments in Time*, which was published by V Press in 2022.

# A TREE AMID THE WOOD

## M. C. Tuggle

THAT woman has come into my house again. I hear her husky voice as she grills my caregiver for anything she can learn about me. Some of the words elude me. The curtains, woven from the translucent leaves of living plants, rustle in the air, distorting the murmurs from the next room.

Often I cannot understand people. My voice is another lost gift. I know what I want to say, but the words will not come. There is a dream that haunts me. I am a boy, maybe six. A man with leathery hands and warm eyes tilts a bucket of young fish into a clear lake. He laughs as I try to catch them in the falling water, but the little silver creatures slip between my fingers.

That's what it's like when I try to grasp the words to express my thoughts.

The mushrooms on the large tree in my bedroom glow yellow-green. So nap time is almost over. In a few minutes, the caregiver will steer my hoverchair into the room and guide me to the kitchen table. The speech teacher will show me pictures and ask me questions. I try to talk, but can only move my lips. He asks yes-or-no questions. If I can't mouth my answer, it's thumbs up for yes, thumbs down for no. And that woman will be there, the one with the searching eyes, with brown hair parted down the middle into two waves, like an eagle about to enfold its prey in its wings.

Me.

She always smiles and acts like she comes here to help. But I know what she's up to. She wants the secret of my house.

I will not let her have it. Sometimes I know what she's asking, but I act like I don't understand. It's my only defense.

The caregiver sweeps the leafy curtain aside, the hoverchair at his side. He smiles, as if he does not know or care he is about to deliver me to a predator.

• • •

While I'm waiting for the caregiver to bring Franklin into the kitchen, Tomás Fuentes, Franklin's speech pathologist, lets himself in. Dark-haired and bearded, he shuts the door behind him and narrows his eyes at me.

"Hello, Carrie."

"Tomás."

"You're early. Looking forward to interrogating your prisoner?"

"You misjudge me, Tomás. I want to help him as much as you do."

"And for the most noble of reasons."

I take a deep breath and remind myself my goal is good. Franklin Pratt's house, once it's mass-produced, will convert greenhouse gasses into living homes. Affordable, sustainable homes.

And yes, this will make money for my client. Franklin left no notes behind, so my client's only hope is to help him speak again.

I open my briefcase and power up a ShoCube. "Can you use this?" A hologram of a boy and woman fills the air before us. The boy peers sideways toward the camera, his eyes sparkling with youthful conspiracy. The woman smiles down at the boy. Dwarf pear trees, their limbs heavy with golden fruit, encircle them. "It's Franklin and his mother."

Tomás squints at the image, eyes darting back and forth, betraying an inner debate. He waves his hand over the image and it dissolves. "This is good. Franklin has no family now, and I couldn't find anyone with mementos like this. He's always been a loner."

"I know."

"This old picture could very well trigger memories." His brow furrows. "And your client could learn how to make a house that communes with its owner and grows rooms and furniture as needed."

"Which will benefit millions."

"And make billions."

I let his little barb go with a shrug. The curtain of leaves covering Franklin's bedroom swishes open, and the caregiver tows Franklin's hoverchair forward. The bioluminescent trees forming the hallway cast a blue aura, perhaps a "Good afternoon" to their creator. The caregiver pauses to let Franklin see them. Does Franklin know what he's looking at? The bony face topped with tangled white hair is a long blank.

Franklin designed this house to psychically connect with its residents so it could respond to their needs and help them feel closer to nature. The psychiatrists my client hired suggested Franklin remain here, hoping the bond would restore his memory.

I see little evidence it's working.

Tomás leans close to me. "Franklin's parents were so antitechnology they wouldn't let him or his sister have cell phones. How did you get that picture?"

"I'm an investigator, Tomás. You told me old pictures can help stroke victims recall lost memories. It took some digging, but I found a childhood friend who'd sneaked a phone onto the farm back in the 20s."

Tomás tries to stifle a smile. "Franklin looks impish in that picture. I'd say his rebellious streak is what led him to leave the farm and study biotechnology. He and his parents never reconciled."

"In his file I read—oh, here they come."

The caregiver parks Franklin between us and excuses himself. We sit at a table of living dogwood, its surface flat, its edges trimmed with heart-shaped leaves.

Tomás sets an artist's sketch pad and crayons in front of Franklin. "Good afternoon, Franklin. Did you have a good nap?"

Franklin does not answer.

Tomás takes a crayon and writes "My Childhood Home" on the first page. "Franklin, I have a special surprise for you. Do you want to see it?"

No response. Tomás motions the ShoCube back on, and the holo of young Franklin and his mother floats over the table.

Franklin regards the scene for nearly a minute. He works his jaw, eyes flickering with life and recognition. His eyes shine with tears. He mouths a word.

As if we'd rehearsed it, Tomás and I say "Mother" in unison. We glance at each other.

"Very good Franklin," says Tomás. "Yes, that was your mother. Do you remember where you are in this picture?"

Franklin grasps the crayon and scrawls "our farm" on the pad.

Tomás takes a deep breath. "Well done, Franklin."

I kneel beside Franklin's hoverchair. Tomás glares at me, starts to speak, but I wave him away. "Franklin, it's Carrie Masada. Do you understand me?"

Thumbs up.

"We don't have much time. You had a stroke. Do you remember?"

Thumbs down.

"You have to believe me," I continue. "You are a generous person who wants to share your gift with the world. When you had the stroke, you forgot who you were. You forgot you wanted others to have houses like this. Your house will do so much good—"

Franklin grimaces, stretches his hand toward the crayon, and grips it. His eyes burn at me as he crushes it against the table.

Tomás raises one eyebrow. "Guess you got your answer."

I did indeed.

• • •

For a moment, she almost won, but I saw what she was doing.

She kept hitting me with questions, but I did not answer. The speech teacher took over, and I pretended not to hear.

They finally gave up for the day.

The night caregiver helps me to bed. The shining blossoms glow, edged in ruby light. My house no doubt senses my lingering anger against that woman. I close my eyes and breathe in night air that smells like rain and moss.

My eyes open. While I slept, the honeysuckle shifted on the ceiling. I gaze up and imagine it's a face. Half-hidden behind the supporting live-oak branches, two hibiscus buds blossom where eyes would be. A woman's eyes. The brown vines beneath them make a strong, pretty nose, and a dark shadow between the rows of ivy transitions into a knowing smile.

Far away, a voice calls. It is a pleasant voice, a woman's voice, the pitch and timbre warm and soothing, yet insistent. It asks a strange question.

She is nowhere to be seen, though her relentless question

is clear: "What is the name of our home?" I open my mouth to answer, but no words come. They escape me, as they often do.

My eyes open, and I search the ceiling above me. Nothing. The comforting image formed by the vines and self-grafting trees has vanished. Self-grafting—that's a term I haven't heard or thought about in some time. The word pleaching returns to me, too, and for a moment I recall how I once weaved together different tree branches to form living structures, structures sustained by walls packed with loam and clay that nourish the trees and insulate the house.

I recognize the voice from my dream. It was my mother.

The answer to her question bubbles up from deep inside, and I say, "Plentywood." The instant I whisper that word to the dark blossoms and vines surrounding me, I recall my mother and father handing out crates of fresh corn, collards, and ripe fruits to grateful neighbours. A wave of recognition radiates through me: the man in my dream pouring fish into the pond is my father. My mother bends close and I turn to her. She says, "Why do we do this? Because we have plenty, and we share it."

My eyes blur, and I clench them shut. I know what I have to do. My fingers find the medical bracelet, and I call the caregiver.

• • •

I return to Franklin's at 8:30 the next morning. The caregiver motions me toward the kitchen table, where Tomás and Franklin are sitting. I do a double-take. Franklin is tapping at a keyboard, and the text appears in the holo.

Tomás announces, "We've had a breakthrough, Carrie. A big one."

"Yes, I see."

"Franklin understands what I say, and he answers on the keyboard. Now he's typing—something else."

I take a chair, expecting to see simple practice sentences. Good thing I'm not standing. I read Franklin's document and slump in my seat, slack-jawed and dizzy. Franklin's text is not only coherent, but highly technical. The instructions for grafting Franklin's living house float before my eyes like a captured dream.

Tomás shoots me a look and exhales. "I'm sure you're happy."

I open my mouth, shut it, and stare. Franklin pecks steadily with two fingers at a keyboard set to the old QWERTY format.

I poke my finger through a paragraph. "Are you reading this?"

Tomás seems fixated on the holographic text.

I rise from my chair, hunch over Franklin's shoulder, and read out loud:

"No idea how much time I have, so I want to thank you for your patience and skill. Thank you, Tomás."

Franklin gazes at Tomás, who glances back, turns, and rubs his eyes.

Franklin types, "And thank you, Carrie."

"You're welcome."

"I have not been myself lately. I had a stroke. Still, I want to apologize."

"Franklin, there's nothing to apologize for."

"Yes, there is. I know I've been difficult, and that I've demanded a lot from people in my life. I want to make things right."

He feels guilty. He has no family to share his feelings with, so I let him type.

"When I resisted you, I thought I was protecting my home. Strange as it may seem, I was even more convinced I had to fight you when I saw the picture from Plentywood."

"Your parents' farm."

Franklin types, "How long have you and Tomás been working on me?"

"About three months."

"Sometimes I couldn't understand you. Sometimes I pretended. Especially in the past few weeks."

"I wondered about that."

"I often heard the banter between you two. I know what it's like to push toward a goal so hard that you alienate others. But remember, Carrie, it takes both good intentions and toughness to do good things."

Now Franklin is trying to justify his life's work, including his hard-driving style.

Or is he? I lower my gaze. My head spins and my thoughts scatter. When I look up, there's a crooked smile on his face.

# ABOUT THE AUTHOR

M. C. Tuggle is a life-long tinkerer and science geek now retired from the insurance industry, where he worked in project management and operations research. His science fiction, fantasy, and mystery stories have been featured in several publications, including *Mystery Weekly*, *Hexagon Speculative Fiction*, and *Metaphorosis*. The Novel Fox published his novella *Aztec Midnight* in 2016, a fantasy adventure based on his extended stay in a Mexican village. He posts his literary opinions at mctuggle.com, and occasionally tweets at @tuggle_mike.

# THE WINDTECH

## Victoria Brun

THE first thing we learn when the windtech arrives is that wind turbines are female—or at least he calls them all "she" for some reason.

"She looks to be in remarkably good shape," he says as he peers through a pair of binoculars at the nearest turbine, which is standing idle in the distance. Its blades haven't turned in years. "The exterior all looks good."

"It doesn't put out any power," one of the townsfolk complains. "It just sullies the view."

A murmur of agreement follows her words. There are about two dozen of us gathered here. The stranger who thinks he can fix the turbines is big news.

"I can probably fix her," he says as he lowers his binoculars to study us. "I just need to get up there to see what the problem is."

"Fix it?" another onlooker echoes. "How are you going

to fix it? It's in the swamp! It's sitting in ten feet of water!"

He grins and looks out over what once was a huge field but is now eternally drenched in salty water. "That's not a problem. She's just an offshore turbine now."

"How you going to get up there?" someone else asks.

"There's a ladder inside. If someone could take me out there on their boat, I could climb it."

This comment elicits a gasp, and more outrage.

"*Climb* it? Boy, you are going to *fall!* You can't climb that!"

His expression and the grey in his beard suggest that he is unused to being called "boy." However, he recovers quickly and forces a smile. "I promise I won't fall." He motions at the duffle bag slung over one broad shoulder. "I've got all the proper safety equipment, and I always use a 100% tie-off."

The townsfolk remain unconvinced. We hold a whispered side conversation, pretending he can't overhear. Everyone proclaims how ridiculous this is—this outsider thinking he can revive the broken turbine.

It's not his fault; he tried his best to convince us. His easy smile, easy demeanour might have appeased other towns, but we're the people who stayed behind, and we're as suspicious as they come.

Most people have moved inward—away from the flooding coasts and country and into the inland cities. Towns like Louisville, Kentucky, and Wichita, Kansas, are now the places to be. They say the new cities are nothing like the old ones. They call them "smart cities" now—and "green cities."

They claim they are clean and safe. And we do not trust them, we who stayed behind in the hot, flooded remains of the New Coast.

"So," the windtech says, interrupting our whispers that have morphed into pure conspiracy theories. "Would anyone be willing to take me?" He motions at the turbine sitting in the swamp.

"You going to charge us?" someone asks. "To fix it?"

He sighs. It's a well-earned sigh, because he's already explained this three times. "No. I'm funded under the RENEW Act. I'm part of a corps of people working to restore—"

"Government," someone interrupts him in a tone laced with distrust. "Working for the government."

"Right," he says. "So no one needs to pay me. But I do need a lift to the turbine. I'm afraid I didn't bring my own boat." He smiles like it's a joke, but we can see he's getting desperate. It's in his eyes.

Several people shrug. A few people leave, wandering off like they suddenly remembered an errand. Some mutter excuses before leaving. Others just laugh at him. They want to see him fail.

"I'll take you," I say, the words leaving my mouth in some strange fashion that seems to have bypassed my brain. Everyone looks at me. His eyebrows arch high with surprise, and I think he'll say something about me just being a kid, but he doesn't. Instead, he grins. It's a real smile this time, without the desperation.

"Thank you," he says.

I lead him to my little jon boat, a flat-bottomed aluminum craft. It's ancient. Probably older than the turbine—but it's held up. He sits in the front, and I sit in the back to steer.

He runs his fingers idly through the water, but I warn him not to. We have alligators, Burmese pythons, and who knows what else in there. He yanks his hand back.

We make small talk over the roar of the motor as we head to the turbine. I casually slip the fact that I just graduated high school into the conversation, so he doesn't think I'm a little kid. Everyone in town seems to think I'm eternally a kid.

He asks me what I'm planning to do next. College? Trade school? Work?

I tell him I don't know, which is the truth.

He says there is a demand for wind technicians. I could do an apprenticeship for it. I just shrug at the suggestion, but I feel a swirl of excitement as we arrive at the base of the idle turbine. There is something exhilarating about this—of doing something.

He stares down into the murky water around its base and sighs. "The access door is under there."

"How you going to get in then?"

"I guess I'm going to get wet." He stuffs his duffle bag into a black garbage bag and knots it. He casts a quick look around the water. "Let's hope I get lucky on the gators."

"I'll watch," I say as I reach for the whistle on my lifejacket. A loud noise *should* scare a gator away, although I don't know what I'll do if I see a python.

The windtech slides over the side of the boat and disappears below its surface with a splash. It's hard to see in the water, but he doesn't resurface, and the water stays calm, so I suppose he must have made it.

I look up, watching the top of the tower, what he called the nacelles. I wait for him to appear, as I nervously tap the side of the boat. When he does, I cheer, and he waves down at me. I wave back.

He's so high up that he looks tiny. I find myself desperately hoping he can revive the old beast. I'm suddenly far more invested in this than in any high school football game.

He had asked me to come back for him in six hours, but I stay nearby and fish. I catch seven fish, but none are even as long as my hand, so I toss them back.

He comes back down in five hours, and swims to my boat. He tosses the garbage bag in first and then hauls himself aboard. Above us, the turbine blades are slowly but victoriously spinning in the breeze. When moving, it is beautiful. I start to understand why he doesn't call the turbine "it." She seems alive.

"You did it!" I lean forward to offer him a high five.

He grins and slaps my hand. "That was a surprisingly easy fix—she really was in good shape. Her brake was just stuck."

"What are you going to do now?" I ask.

"On to the next turbine," he says as he wrings water from his shirt. Or tries to. "And then to the next town. I'm just going to keep heading south down the coast."

"Think you'll need a boat?" I ask.

He rubs a hand along his nape. "Yeah. I reckon I might."

"I could come," I offer. "If you need a hand. Or an apprentice?"

He smiles again. "I think that could be arranged."

# ABOUT THE AUTHOR

Victoria Brun is a writer and project manager at a national laboratory. When not bugging hardworking scientists about budget reports and service agreements, she is daydreaming about futuristic worlds, aliens, and magic. Her other short fiction includes pieces at *Daily Science Fiction, Uncharted Magazine*, and beyond. Find her on Twitter at @VictoriaLBrun.

# AN INTERSECTION OF PARALLEL LIVES

## Wendy Nikel

"You don't need a reason to save people," I argue to the boss. But apparently, if I'm flying on her dime, I do.

In the end, it's the chickens that win her over. The records I uncovered deep in the archives state that two centuries ago, when the *Novus* and its passengers departed to colonize H3985, they carried with them two dozen hens and five roosters. Science has railgunned itself ahead since the generation ship left on its voyage across the galaxy, but even with nutrient tablets making food superfluous now for human survival, there's plenty of Old-World purists who'd pay trillions for a bite of a bite of a genuine, nonsynthetic drumstick.

It's all about the bottom line. Supply and demand. Upward-sloping graphs of profit margins.

With the boss's permission finally given, I slip into my sleek *Raptor* (a thousand times faster than the largely forgotten *Novus*), and point its nose toward the dot of sky where I hope to find the lost ship—a sliver of space that the experts have collectively decided isn't actually that promising after all, revenue-wise.

As I fire up the engines, I think of the other discovery I'd made in the archives. The information I didn't share. A record of an ancestor—sharing my surname, my blood—who'd deserted Earth, though his pregnant wife refused to. A broken family. A connection severed. A monumental choice by two people I'd never met that, like the earth growing smaller behind my ship, grew smaller in significance as time marched on, until that one life-altering decision became nothing more than a dot on the timeline of my family history. And yet, like the earth falling out of sight somewhere below, that one dot makes all the difference.

The boss checks in on the communications link on day seventy-one of eighty-two. There's nothing to boost the signal between here and there, so her voice sounds thin and awash in static. She's second-guessing now, anxious about what I'll find. What life has become aboard the isolated *Novus*, if life still exists there at all. She makes me promise that if the inhabitants have resorted to cannibalism, I'll grab a few chickens and get out, ASAP.

"Get the chickens," she reiterates. That's the important part, all logic aside.

On day eighty-one, a dot appears in the distance. I spend

the day staring at it across the expanse. When I wake from my next sleep cycle, the cylindrical ship looms in my window. I've found it.

I slow the *Raptor* to match its speed. Apprehension, excitement, and determination combat in my chest, crowding out my breath. Here's what I've waited for since first uncovering the records. Since first wondering "what if?" What if *I'd* spent my life stuck in a jettisoned tin can, in a civilization spent spinning slowly toward somewhere I'd die without reaching? In rescuing the *Novus*, I was rescuing that could've-been me, too. In my own way, I've warped the timeline, doubled back upon my family's past, so that these lives, which for the past two centuries have run parallel, now have the chance to intersect.

The *Raptor* hatch was retrofitted before we left, and it slides easily into the *Novus*'s dock. I pause, stop, catch my breath. This is my moment: the moment of intersection. Of truth. How will history describe it to those further down this temporal line? Will they know the bravery it requires, approaching this amputated limb of humanity?

The airlock swings open, and the air that greets me is fresh. *Clean.*

"Goodness gracious, are you OK?" The woman standing before me looks strong. Bright-eyed. Healthy. Kind.

Behind her, the ship opens to a jungle of lush flora, the likes of which haven't been seen on Earth for decades. There are trees here, taller and thicker than any I'd ever seen, and vines and grasses and shrubbery, too. Men and women pass beyond the leaves, speaking softly to one another. Laughing. Smiling. A chicken rushes unhindered across a moss-covered path, followed by a trail of fluff-feathered chicks. I stare, dumbfounded at the tiny creatures.

"Someone get this pilot a cot; she's dazed." The woman taps an unfamiliar device to my forehead and frowns. "Dehydration, malnourishment, and hypertension. Lots of toxicity in her bloodstream as well. Get her something to eat, STAT, and then we'll see what we can do about the rest."

I brace myself as I'm surrounded, but what falls upon me is not the cold touch of shiny-armed med-bots subtracting credits for care prepayment. It's gentle human voices, gentle human arms, and gentle human faces guiding me to the softest bed I've ever felt. Water trickles down my throat, tasting strange and sweet without the familiar chemical sting. Music floats in the air, unhampered by screeching newsfeeds or the periodic advertising blurb. Even the scents are softer— more subtle and easier on my throat.

Everything is so … peaceful.

"Good thing we were here to save you."

I look up. The surname on the woman's badge matches mine. Her eyes bear the same shape and colour as my own.

"Yes." I realize then with sharp, sudden clarity. "It is."

# ABOUT THE AUTHOR

Wendy Nikel is a speculative fiction author with a degree in elementary education, a fondness for road trips, and a terrible habit of forgetting where she's left her cup of tea. Her short fiction has been published by *Analog*, *Nature Futures*, *Podcastle*, and elsewhere. Her time travel novella series, beginning with *The Continuum*, is available from World Weaver Press. For more info, visit wendynikel.com.

# SPECIATION FOR THE NEW MILLENNIUM

## Jon Hansen

EVERYONE was thrilled at the radon building up
in the cellars, slowly staining our children's skins
until they shimmered and radiated and shone.
"Look what a healthy glow they have," we cried. "Besides,
it makes it easier to tuck them in at night."

And few minded more arsenic in the water
even after our children grew fat poison sacs
and spat venom at us if we sent them to bed
without any supper. "It's a tough world," we said.
"Better than mace. They just need to learn some restraint."

And no one said anything when the power plants
pumped out more $CO_2$ and our children budded,
sprouting little leaves and curled vines in their hair.
"Photosynthesis is a useful trade," we mused.
"Make no mistake. Besides, they look so cute in green."

And we just smiled when the pondering slowness of
global warming melted the poles and our children
opened their new gills and withdrew beneath the waves.
"It's always sad to see them leave home," we sighed.
"Even when we worked so hard to bring them up right."

## ABOUT THE AUTHOR

Jon Hansen (he/his) is a writer, former librarian, and
occasional blood donor. He lives about fifty feet from Boston
with his wife, son, and three pushy cats. His short fiction and
poetry have appeared in a variety of places, including *Strange
Horizons*, *Daily Science Fiction*, and *Lady Churchill's Rosebud
Quarterly*. Like many these days, he's working on a novel,
when not spending too much time on Twitter. He likes tea
and cheese.

# THE INEVITABLIST

## David Lee Zweifler

IT was called Moon Base Daintree, but it was less a base than a tube. A long, subway-car-sized tube, with a hatch at either end.

Inside was a conference table, life support, and a fridge filled with refreshments—in case the alien was humanoid.

Preston Jorgenson paced his end of the tube as the alien ship completed its intricate docking procedure at the other.

There was, certainly, a lot riding on this meeting, but Preston was sure that nobody else on Earth had his acumen or negotiation skills.

He knew he would get a deal done.

The alien made Preston nervous, though. Their civilization had sent humanity nothing but audio communications so, for the first time in decades, Preston wasn't much better informed about what the future held than anyone else back on Earth.

*What would he or she look like?* Preston wondered. *Would it be a terrifying xenomorph like in Alien with sharp edges and spikes, or a gorgeous green-skinned woman like the Orion girls in Star Trek?*

This visit was to determine whether the aliens would share their technology. They claimed they could help humanity repair the earth, enabling it to survive the climate apocalypse already in full swing. Or they could abandon it to its fate.

"Your society will need to band together, pooling its innovation and its resources, to build a base on your moon where you will meet our emissary in three years' time," said the synthesized voice at the end of the alien message, which they broadcast globally, in all languages, nearly thirty-six months ago.

When Preston heard that message, he knew what he needed to do. Governments had been completely ineffectual in dealing with climate issues. Preston was the world's first trillionaire. Without the help of the aliens, he would probably be its last.

"I've never been a big fan of 'pooling,'" he had said at his press conference the next day. "As you know, I'm an inevitablist. If something is going to happen, if it's unavoidable, I believe you need to embrace the change, even if it's painful or disruptive.

"Representative governments don't have the resources, efficiency, or innovation to handle this mission," Preston continued. "It's inevitable that a private enterprise will take the lead. As CEO of Daintree, I feel like this challenge falls to us in particular. We will build the moon base and deliver me there as Earth's emissary in three years' time."

Since then, the creation of the Daintree moon base had progressed at a breakneck pace.

There was some pushback by world leaders and governments angry about Daintree relegating them to the background or shutting them out completely.

"You're free to build your own rocket and your own moon base," Preston had told the president and the Joint Chiefs of Staff in one of the early planning meetings. "But don't expect Daintree to give away its skills or resources to the competition."

After Preston brought intense lobbying and other pressures to bear, the U.S. government and all the rest eventually fell into line, giving him the tax breaks, the clearances, and everything else … right down to the naming rights on the station.

*That's a billion-dollar piece of marketing for Daintree right there,* Preston thought. *I might even turn a profit on saving the world.*

The clanging of the alien ship docking with the moon base had stopped. Preston considered putting his hands down on the meeting-room table, pushing his upper chest forward, and spreading his legs slightly in a pose that conveyed confidence and power, like a potent, silverback gorilla.

*Maybe just a bit too aggressive,* he thought.

He adjusted, putting his left hand flat on the table, and the other on his hip, turning his head slightly to the left, like a majestic swan. *More casual. But perhaps giving a hint of impatience.*

Preston went to adjust again but, midgesture, the alien's hatch opened, startling him, and leaving him, for a fraction of a second, in a pose like a frightened donkey.

"Hey there handsome," the alien said.

He was neither a xenomorph nor a green-skinned girl. He was Preston. Same face. Same body. Same voice. Even the same stylish space suit that Preston was wearing now.

"What … how …?" Preston stuttered.

"It's probably a bit disconcerting to see a duplicate of yourself," the alien said. "They custom design the emissary to match the representative they're speaking to. When they made me, they toyed with the idea of making me look like your father, or some other loved one to put you at ease. The computer determined that this image was the one that you had the most positive associations with, so we went with it."

"What … what are you?" Preston asked. "Does your species shape-shift?"

"What? Me? No. I'm not one of … you know. Them." The alien gestured towards his end of the tube, and the ship. "I'm a single-use organism. They designed me using your genetic code to negotiate just for this meeting on their behalf. My mind, such as it is, uses an analysis of every public interaction you've ever had, and every electronic communication—every record of everything that you've ever said or written, public and private. If I may, I'd just like to say how much I enjoyed your autobiography. *The Inevitablist*—great stuff!"

"So, you're … me?" Preston asked.

"Mostly." The alien shrugged. "Who knows? Does anyone ever really know anyone?"

"To be clear, you're authorized to negotiate on behalf of … I don't know what to call them."

"'Them' is fine."

"Doesn't your creators' species have a name?"

"Let's see how things go, OK?"

"Well, I guess that means all my fancy negotiation strategies go right out the window." Preston relaxed a bit.

Then, he tensed: "Look, you know me, and you know our situation. It's dire. Please … please help me. Help us."

"I appreciate you worked hard to get here, and to create this … tube."

"It's a moon base!" Preston couldn't help getting a bit frustrated. Wired Magazine had derisively called it a "tube" as well.

"Moon base. Yes. As I said, you worked hard, so we came here out of respect. But we were pretty clear with the directions. You didn't follow them. So I'm afraid the answer is no."

A silence settled into the hollow space, interrupted only by the sudden humming of the machine that recycled carbon dioxide back into breathable air.

"Sorry?" asked Preston. "What?"

"I'm afraid the answer is no," the alien repeated.

"But we did what you asked."

"The exercise was designed to force the disparate peoples of Earth—across cultures, across geographies—to work together, sacrifice together, and innovate together to create a technology here on the moon."

"We did that. We just did it with Daintree," Preston said.

"Yes. Getting the naming rights was a nice touch," the alien said. "But creating a tube ... I'm sorry. I meant 'moon base' ... having it done through a for-profit entity under the direction of one man defeats the whole purpose of the exercise."

"What difference does it make who built it, how many, or where they're from?" Preston asked.

"You know, we have the technology to fix your planet, but you'll be back in the soup again in two hundred years unless people stop being so selfish, and work together," the alien said. "This moon base exercise was meant to be the first step—an important signal that humanity was ready to make the change. But you couldn't even do that right."

For a moment, Preston was without words.

"Look," Preston said, "humans may not be as technologically superior as your people—"

"You're not," the alien interrupted.

"—but we have art, film, music. Our diversity and beauty could add value to your culture."

"Humans are also arrogant, resentful ... dangerous," the alien said. "I'm pretty sure that your diversity and beauty are not worth the risk."

"We have to have something you want," Preston pleaded. "I mean ... water? Air? Gold?"

Now it was the alien's turn to pause.

"Yes." The alien sighed. "We do value those things. And I hate to be mean, but why barter with you people now, when we can just, you know, wait"—the alien took out a sheet of paper from his pocket—"thirty-two years? That's how long your species has got. After that, we can just come down and … well … take it."

"That's bullshit! We'll survive. We'll fight you!" Preston collected himself. "We can change. We'll pull together and do what we have to do to survive. We don't need you."

"Listen, Preston," the alien said. "You're me. And I'm you. So, believe me when I tell you this doesn't make me happy. I love you, man. I love all humans. But the fact is, this was kind of the last chance. And it feels bad to feel like you've blown it. I get it …"

"I haven't …" Preston started.

"Please," the alien said. "Let me finish. Like you said to the president: nobody would have even made it up here to the moon if it wasn't for you. And, so, in a way, you've shown that you're a boss. That you will rise to the top even in the most difficult situations. Even when there's no chance of winning."

Preston processed this.

"Is there anything? Anything at all we can do to show you that we're worthy of your help?" Preston asked.

"I guess you can say I'm an inevitablist too," the alien said. "There's some painful, disruptive change coming. The best thing you can do right now is to embrace it."

"You're me, right?" Preston asked. "Look, man, do me a

solid. You've got to give me something. Something I can take back to Earth."

The alien Preston stared at him for a long while. "Obviously, the truth isn't going to fly."

The alien moved towards the hatch to his ship.

"Honestly," the alien turned back suddenly. "If I were you, I'd say that the aliens are sending help but in the meantime, you're giving everyone a $20 gift card for Daintree."

Preston laughed without mirth at his counterpart's insight. Free stuff and a few words of hope were probably all it would take for everyone to embrace the inevitable.

# ABOUT THE AUTHOR

David Lee Zweifler worked as a reporter and marketer in jobs that took him around the world, including long stints in Jakarta, Hong Kong, and New York City. Most of those roles had him chronicling the evolution of AI, showing how it was changing things for the better, the worse, and the weirder. The last is a thread that runs through much of David's fiction today. David's work appears in *Little Blue Marble*, *The Dread Machine*, and *Wyldblood*, and he has upcoming stories in *Analog* and Shortwave Media's *Obsolescence* anthology. His website is davidleezweifler.com. His Twitter handle is @dzweifler.

# WHAT TO EXPECT WHEN YOU'RE EXPECTING ADVANCED LIFE-FORMS

## Jason A. Bartles

BEFORE becoming a plarent, I dedicated most of my energy to sculpting the contours of my crust and pumping up my magnetic fields. I was young and gorgeous—the envy of my siblings—living my best life in the fast lane. As the ages passed, however, a sense of emptiness overcame me. Then came the bad years. The sun flared up relentlessly, and Saturn taunted me with their shiny rings. I acted out. I said some things that could not be unsaid to the moon. After they turned their back on me, I fell into a dark place. Luckily, with some time to process, I had an epiphany: I said to myself, Earth, you need someone to love and care for. You need to develop those simple organisms spawning in your waters into advanced life-forms. My siblings dismissed it as another of my eccentricities. A cry for attention. But once they caught sight of the dinosaurs, it was all anyone would talk about.

Raising advanced life is a struggle at times, but trust me, you'll experience a joy like no other. I admit I have not been perfect. You're surely familiar with my current plight. That's why I started this newsletter: to share my best tips with all the other expecting plarents out there.

## BE PROACTIVE

Don't wait around for a rogue asteroid or for another plarent's life-forms to go viral. Stay true to your authentic self. Cultivate the simple organisms that come naturally to you. Throw a little radiation their way. Pit the strongest survivors against one another. Surprise them with a natural disaster. The fun lies in seeing how they respond to catastrophic change.

## EMBRACE YOUR THICK ATMOSPHERE

Everyone wants to flaunt their deepest valleys and highest peaks, but don't get caught up in the hype. Advanced life-forms thrive under a dense, protective atmosphere. Plus, it hides the endless heaps of garbage from the prying eyes of your neighbours.

## PREPARE FOR EXTINCTION-LEVEL EVENTS

Not a day goes by that I don't think about the dinosaurs.

After the meteor, I fell into a deep depression and shrouded myself in darkness. I was desperate to replace those majestic reptiles with a species that would not remind me of them, and I have been paying for it ever since.

## DO NOT MEMORIALIZE

Do not convert the final remains of your life-forms into combustibles. Do not let them well up to the surface. Do not entrust them to deep underground deposits. The primates will find them. They will exhume and burn them because they know you loved the dinosaurs more.

## AVOID PRIMATES

They are capable of love and charity, yet too many of them cling to fear and revel in destructive behaviours. I'm partially to blame, letting them evolve when I was in such an unstable phase. Right now, I cannot wait for them to be gone. But who knows? Maybe I'll remember them more fondly once I have a chance to cool off.

# ABOUT THE AUTHOR

Jason A. Bartles is a queer SFF writer and professor. Originally from West Virginia, he now calls Philadelphia home. He lives with his husband and two dogs, a blue-eyed husky and a pit-mix who will lick your face off. His fiction has appeared or is forthcoming in *Daily Science Fiction*, *Utopia*

*Science Fiction*, *Metaphorosis*, and as part of the collectively written fantasy clifi anthologies, *The World's Revolution*.

# UNPREDICTABLE WEATHER PATTERNS

## Leigh-Anne Burley

KEVIN isn't like the other members of his notorious family:
his storm-front brothers racing out of the northeast.

Nor is he in the category of his boisterous hurricane cousins,
foaming and churning off the coast.

Kevin isn't even like his howling tornado twin sisters,
twisting and shouting all over the plains.

He is just an insignificant, small storm,
soon to be forgotten.

Even the neighbours don't want to hang out,
thinking Kevin will never amount to much.

Kevin reasons if I can't be a big bad storm
then I will be the best little one. But how?

After studying the others, he notices they are mostly predictable:
racers fly in from the northeast,
brutes rush the coastlines and
twisters spin out on the plains.
Kevin concludes he will fly out in all directions.

He practices spinning fast and turning sharply.
His family thinks he has lost his way.
Eventually, he catches the eye of weather forecasters
who can't keep up with his many surprises.

Kevin delights in playing hide-and-seek by keeping folks
guessing where he will show up next.
Even his family takes notice of his pictures in the news
(all storms love their pictures taken).

Over time, he makes a name for himself as the Ninja Storm,
the most unpredictable weather pattern.
No one knows where he will strike next and
Kevin isn't telling.

# ABOUT THE AUTHOR

Leigh-Anne Burley was born in Toronto, Ontario, Canada, and resides in Virginia with her husband of 42 years She has three children and six grandchildren. Leigh-Anne has a BA in English and MA in Pastoral Counseling. She is published in nonfiction, fiction, and poetry. Leigh-Anne enjoys walking and hiking in nature, reading and writing.

# TREEHOUSE

## Lorraine Schein

THE sky roofs over the Earth house.

Its walls are air,
the floor is soil
where trees and flowers live.

Birds fly through its clear windows
glistening with rain
and perch chattering on the armchairs of trees
to watch the latest changing clouds.

In the bathroom,
icebergs melt in the tub.

Polar bears huddle on slippery ice floes,
gaze down at their mirrored reflections,
brush their teeth and floss.

In the living room,
the shag carpet is alive
with flowers petaling pinks and bugs crawling.

The sea is a water bed,
sloshing with fish inside,
floating clumps of plastic,
and slick brown oil spills.

Everything smells smoky
from wildfires and smog.

Let's clean house—
blast the wind through
to sweep away the debris and tainted air
with brooms of sunlight and hope.

Open the roof to the stars,
so they can move in from the sky
and we can look once more
through clear windows of rain.

# ABOUT THE AUTHOR

Lorraine Schein is a NY writer. Her work has appeared in *VICE Terraform*, *Strange Horizons*, *Mermaids Monthly*, and *New Myths*. Her stories are in the anthologies *Tragedy Queens* and *Wild Women*. *The Futurist's Mistress*, her poetry book, is available from mayapplepress.com. Her latest book is *The Lady Anarchist Café* (Autonomedia), a collection of poetry and science fiction.

# A SEA OF PLASTIC

## Bo Balder

THE sun was barely up over the plastic sea, but it was already stifling hot. The almost horizontal rays bounced off the bleached, matted remnants of last century's excesses. The great raft housing the plastic reclamation factory chewed slowly but steadily through them. Phlox checked her diving gear. If she dove off the back, she had plenty of time to gather samples before the current generated by the big slurping maw in front got too strong. Her spotter Jor had the day off, but she'd done this hundreds of times now. It should be safe enough.

Phlox turned on her phone timer and slid into the water. The safety line paid out behind her automatically. She used her glove and shoe claws to wrestle through the ten-foot-thick layer of bleached debris, milk jugs, dish-liquid bottles, and plastic bags. Finally the plastic thinned out, enough that she could see a couple of yards between the swirling plastic bits. She floated facedown for a bit to cool off. A last check of air, her spear and olona net, and then she dialed up the weights and went down.

The milky green before her eyes became clearer. The coastal waters here were very shallow, or the plastic reclamation factory on its raft wouldn't have been able to manage. Phlox activated her vibrospear and slowly swam through lukewarm water, her knees almost clipping the bottom. Fish had begun to repopulate the seas, and her grant allowed her to catch a couple every month for research purposes. And if these fish, after being weighed and DNA sequenced and necropsied, also got eaten, nobody minded. It was a way of fitting in with the raft crew.

Phlox spotted movement in the corner of her eye and undulated after it, spear in her right hand, net in the left. She would spear a fish if it was big and a species she hadn't seen before, but she preferred to catch them alive.

There it went.

A whirl of plastic bags floated across her goggles and she lost the fish. She was now drifting over a stand of bleached, dead fan coral. She'd seen it so many times before, and it was never not sad. What was left of humanity was working hard to restore the earth, but sometimes knowing it wouldn't happen in her lifetime was hard to bear.

A flicker of movement.

There it was again, the same fish. Or another, that hardly mattered.

Phlox kicked once, gently, and let herself drift over a dull-white brain coral hump. Slowly, slowly, she fanned out her left arm and flicked the net. She used the spear to startle the fish and drove it straight into the net.

A young golden tilefish. Great! Once plentiful and used for sushi—not that Phlox had ever eaten any but the printed kind—its population had dwindled. It was thought they'd disappeared, at least here in the Gulf.

But then Phlox caught sight of a purple leaf shape. Could it be? Without noticing, she let go of her spear and net and hovered over the delicate veined lattice . It was a living fan coral, blooming tenderly among brain and fan coral skeletons, white guardians around the new life.

Phlox didn't know how long she floated, mesmerized by the sight of the living leaf. So pretty. So long awaited and unexpected.

A roil of current shook her out of her trance. The sucking maw of the plastic factory was too close, she could feel it churning. If she didn't get out of here right now, she'd be sucked in.

Where was her spear? Where was her net? Nowhere. Forget them, she didn't have time to find them—

She had to get moving.

A slow thunder thrummed through her bones. No time to wait. She grabbed her line and turned off the first weight. She didn't float up as she expected. The current was already stronger than her buoyancy. And she hadn't even thought to snap a picture!

Phlox turned off all her weights and hauled herself up the

line hand over hand. The tether slipped through her hands without resistance, unmoored. That was bad. No texted SOS would reach the suction crew in time. She had to save herself. She bobbed up against plastic remnants, clawed at them fruitlessly, and got nowhere.

She had to stay calm.

She just had to find a softer spot to punch through the layer of trash. The suction tugged against her harder and harder. Her claws couldn't get traction on the hard, brittle undersides of gallon containers. She was going to die. That couldn't happen, not with such news.

A green light shone over Phlox. At the last possible moment her hands pushed deep into softness. Thank god, the underside of the raft's kitchen garden. She found the web of lines that kept the seaweed together. Just cut it and swim upward, and she'd be safe in no time.

She wanted to tell everyone the good news, she wanted to shout it out. And then she had to go straight back down and document her find with pictures. The restoration was working! Earth would live again.

# ABOUT THE AUTHOR

Bo lives and works close to Amsterdam. Bo is the first Dutch author to have been published in *F&SF* and *Clarkesworld*. Her fiction has also appeared in *Escape Pod*, *Nature*, and other places. Her SF novel *The Wan* was published by Pink Narcissus Press.

For more about her work, you can visit www.boukjebalder.nl or find Bo on Facebook at www.facebook.com/bo.balder.

# THE TRIALS OF THE
# *THORSTEN HAUGEN*

## J. G. Follansbee

CAPTAIN Matt Peasley paced the bridge of the bulk carrier *Thorsten Haugen*, his low-top hard-sole shoes wearing a path on the painted deck. The relative quiet of his ship, compared to times when its engines ran at full throttle, unnerved him. Speed mattered in the shipping business, and in the past, the thrumming of the turbines had reassured him that the old girl would deliver on its promise of profit.

Outside the window, on the sun-drenched weather deck that stretched 200 metres to the bow, four newly installed wing sails offered no such promise. At least not yet.

Matt sipped his scalding cup of black coffee. He glanced at the navigation console, the radar image showing the California coast thirty kilometres to starboard. The speed read 10.5 knots. He let go a heavy sigh and ran his fingers over his walrus mustache, pulling gently on the salt-and-pepper hairs, a nervous habit. He keyed the walkie-talkie hanging on his yellow safety vest. "Sally, can you come to the bridge?"

Beyond the bridge—the brain of *Thorsten Haugen*—the sight of the wing sails rising eighty metres from the deck like giant playing cards put Matt in mind of his great-grandfather Ambrose, founder of the Peasley Line. He wondered what the old man would've made of the airfoils designed by his great-great-grandaughter, Sally Peasley. A. A. Peasley was one of the last Down East sailors, trained on the water from age fourteen. He knew wind and sea as well as the albatross and dolphins he called his shipmates. Almost two centuries had passed since the line's founding after the Civil War, but the necessity for profit hadn't changed. Without it, a man's work was a slow spiral to failure.

To make a profit, Ambrose took risks. His was among the first shipping companies to switch operations from sail to coal-fired steam. Matt's refit of the *Thorsten Haugen* to meet the demands of a warming world risked everything Ambrose and his descendants had built over five generations.

"Yes, Dad?" Sally appeared next to Matt, breaking his train of thought. "I'm coding a few changes to the trim algorithm."

"I need at least another knot and a half out of those sails." Matt gestured forward. "Otherwise, this little experiment won't work."

"I'm doing everything I can." Sally's voice rose. Her shoulders shifted in her oversized coveralls. "The system works. I just need to tweak it."

"You promised twelve knots for two hours."

Two years previous, during Sally's presentation of her refit proposal, a board member wondered whether her simulation could predict actual results on an ocean that didn't care about software or statistics.

"We've got three hours left in the test, Dad. We'll meet the benchmarks."

"It might be three hours until I have to tell the board that this whole project is done and the company is done. We can't go back to bunker oil. How are people supposed to get their AI-powered Chinese washing machines or mind-reading teddy bears for the kids?"

"We've talked about this a hundred times. This is our best chance to cut our fuel use and emissions and keep the government happy."

"It doesn't mean a damn thing if I can't get this old girl to go a little faster."

"You care only about speed, Dad. I'm doing this to save the planet."

"That's not fair, Sally. I care about the planet too. But everyone's got to make a living, and right now, I feel like mine is slipping away."

Matt's throat tightened and his face flushed. He was master of a modest, proud shipping line, and he hated to show the kind of emotion that others might take as weakness. The bridge crew stared ahead, but they were listening. They worried about their jobs, and so did he. He cleared his throat and took another sip of the now lukewarm coffee.

Sally touched his arm. "Dad, we can do this."

So much confidence in those steel-grey eyes. That was one of the things Matt loved about his only child. Sally's mother Annie had given him a gift beyond treasure. Sally put her Berkeley education and her talent for machine learning to work designing a wind-assist system that just might save the family business. Matt understood nothing about the technology, beyond the basics of how wind flowing over an airfoil pulled a ship forward. But when Sally spoke of the promise of wind in the twenty-first century, he heard Annie's voice. He could do nothing but acquiesce. It helped that the numbers added up, at least on paper. He only wished Annie could've lived to see the result.

Matt faced his daughter and spoke quietly. "Yes, I know you can do it, sweetheart, but we're running out of time."

"I'm going back to my office. Don't worry, Dad."

*Don't worry! How is that possible?* The worry started the day his father died. One moment Matt was playing shortstop on his college's basement-dwelling team, the next, he was the heir to a shipping company barely holding its own. The board wanted him to take over, but he resisted. *Do I want Father's tantrums, his eighty-hour weeks, the high blood pressure that killed him?* Then Matt met Annie, and the world was lighter on his shoulders, more manageable, though the worry never went away.

A quarter century later, the final challenge arrived with an email from a government friend. It warned Matt of the regulation about to be published in the Federal Register applying the new carbon tax to bunker oil, the life's blood of ocean shipping. The new tax burden would kill the Peasley Line, unless he adapted.

Matt remembered standing in front of a life-size portrait of Poppy Ambrose in his high-pressure cap and determined expression. He asked the old man, *What shall I leave to Sally? Failure? Or something new?*

Sally gave her presentation to the board with Ambrose's portrait behind her. The Peasley Line would install her bespoke wing sails on *Thorsten Haugen*, the oldest ship in the fleet, and give it new life. Her engines would remain, but they'd only be used when winds were unfavourable or to maneuver in port. Matt swore the old man nodded his approval.

The recirculated, homogenized air of the bridge felt as oppressive to Matt as the stale coffee. Donning his hard hat, Matt stepped out on the bridge wing into the sunshine. On land, the sun would've burned like an oven, but at sea, the wind softened its heat to a pleasant warmth. Matt lifted his binoculars, scanning the weather deck with its red hatches. The wing sails added grace to the otherwise workmanlike lines of a ship never meant to host wind power. He inhaled the same air Ambrose might have breathed, watching a gull hover over the nearest sail, the bird enjoying the vortices that spun off its tip. He envied the bird its freedom.

"Dad," Matt's radio squawked. "Bring *Haugen* into the wind a degree. We're up to Force 5. That'll give us more energy."

Noting how the wind took the tops off the waves, Matt gave the order. Almost imperceptibly, the *Thorsten Haugen* changed course, and Matt saw the wing sails' flaps adjust. He felt the change in his legs, spread slightly to maintain balance as the vessel rode the long swell. Matt ducked back into the bridge and watched the ship's speed rise. In a few minutes, it plateaued at 11.9 knots.

Matt grinned at the helmsman. "The old girl still has some kick!"

An hour passed, then thirty minutes more. Matt was elated. This damned thing might work, he thought. Then, just as *Thorsten Haugen* glided past a headland off her beam, the wind dropped perceptibly. The vessel's speed slowed to 11.4, then 10.5, then a paltry nine knots.

The clock showed the test was done.

Sally appeared, her stricken face revealing her fear and disappointment. "Dad, I didn't expect the wind to drop off like that. The forecast—"

"I've never known a marine forecast worth the paper it's printed on," Matt frowned, feeling as if he'd just stepped off a roller coaster. So much of life on the water was unpredictable. But if family was steady, if work gave you satisfaction, and you could enjoy a sunrise on the open water, then all was well.

"I didn't keep my promise. Twelve knots for two hours. What will you tell the board?" Sally's eyes glistened.

Matt glanced into his empty coffee cup and sighed. He

imagined himself delivering the news to the board; he wouldn't let Sally humiliate herself. She'd worked too hard, and he still believed in her. What's more, he wasn't ready to give up just because an arbitrary measurement didn't come out quite right in a world where uncertainty was the norm. He'd do the human thing and take the risk.

"You're forgetting something, sweetheart. I'm the captain of this ship, and I decide what is success, and what isn't."

Sally's brow furrowed, another ghost gesture of Annie's.

"I'm calling the sea trials of the wing sails a success. Maybe by a hair's breadth, but a win is a win."

Sally hugged her father, and Matt, watching the growing smile on the helmsman's face, let himself return the embrace.

"We do have to fix one thing aboard this ship," Matt said. "This coffee has to go. Poppy Ambrose would never allow it."

# ABOUT THE AUTHOR

J.G. Follansbee is a Seattle-based writer published in *Bards and Sages Quarterly, Children, Churches and Daddies,* and the anthologies *Satirica, After the Orange, Still Life 2018, Spring Into SciFi 2019, Rabbit Hole II, Sunshine Superhighway, Fix the World,* and *Extinction Notice: Tales of a Warming Earth.* He is the author of the series *Tales From A Warming Planet* and the trilogy *The Future History of the Grail.* He has won several awards in the Writers of the Future contest, and he was a finalist in the inaugural Aftermath short story contest. He also has numerous nonfiction book credits.

# FORWARD MOMENTUM AND A PARALLEL TOSS

## AnaMaria Curtis

ON the marching-band field, everything echoes of Alex. Lacey's students spread across the sideline and cue their robots, and Lacey sees herself as a teenager in a giant sweatshirt, Alex next to her, looks at the bots and remembers Alex's head on hers when she curled up around him in the last row of the bus, talking through choreography. But those are the wrong kinds of memories to have of Alex, so Lacey swallows down nostalgia and focuses on the field, looking for tiny errors to focus on at the next practice. They're going to win regionals today, but state will be harder.

The robots roll onto the field, music swelling from speakers, each robot an individual instrument, and she looks for Edsel and Amber, each on one end of the line of students, wearing their blue cocaptain armbands, holding the manual override controls. To the left of Amber is Bruin, in his yellow and green JM sweatshirt and baseball cap, shoulders straight, and Lacey sees Alex there too, the unfortunate heart of the problem she was never able to solve.

She sits in the stands, unusual for a coach, but everyone has their whims, and watches her students absolutely steamroll over the competition. Their bass drums have real arms and drums instead of speakers, and twelve of their robots can do a parallel toss, their long, oddly jointed arms making precise work of the back-to-front transition and the proud whirl of colour overhead. The other teams have no chance.

They'll have to stay for the exhibition performance now, which Lacey resents despite herself, but the exhibition is all the kids—she doesn't even know what its final form looks like—so she sneaks off to get some ice cream while they're preparing for it.

As she goes to pay, a man in a long-sleeved JM shirt puts his sundae next to hers and says he's paying, and Lacey turns to argue, but then she sees it's Alex.

"What the hell are you doing here?" she asks, when they're safely in a deserted high-school hallway, invisible to the teams scurrying around to pack up and prepare for the awards and exhibition. Her ice cream is melting into its biodegradable bowl.

"I volunteered to be a JM recruiter for regionals," he says. "Hoped to catch you and thought the ice cream stand was my surest bet." His grin unfurls like an open secret, and for a second Lacey doesn't begrudge him being right.

But mostly seeing him just makes her sad. "What do you want, Alex?"

And just like that the grin is gone. "I wanted to warn you to settle down a little," he says, sticking his thumb through a belt loop, looking anywhere but at her. "JM sales in Madrid" —he winks—"comma Illinois, have been going down since you came back and started coaching the band, and now some people are trying to get out of their contracts early. I don't want to have to do any digging into the reason why, but you understand I have my suspicions." He says "Madrid" like a local, the A pronounced long and flat as in apple.

"JM's a big company. I don't think a few counties buying less equipment is going to wreck your profit margins."

Alex chews on his lip, and Lacey reads it all on his face. JM's weaker than it looks. All the sales matter to them right now.

"Competition?" she offers after a moment. "Trouble in corporate paradise?"

Alex scowls and avoids the question. "Everyone in Madrid is growing vegetables, Lacey. And you and I both know people aren't planting acres of carrots and beets by hand."

She shrugs. "They could be. I don't know much about planting." A lie. She's learned a lot the last few years. "Honestly, Alex, 'the band' is literally just twenty-some teenagers looking to practice coding and make robots do funny stuff with their metal limbs. We're no threat."

"All I'm saying is, it would look a lot better if some of the kids from the band were a little more interested in JM contracts. It's good money. And it would help if the sales numbers in the area went up."

"And if they don't?"

There are bags under Alex's eyes and lines on his forehead. He exudes weariness. When he speaks, it's with a sadness that makes Lacey think of a seed, buried deep in dark blocks of soil, of fingers beyond its control pressing it into place.

"Then JM's going to investigate, and they're going to find something, and they're going to prosecute the hell out of it." He sighs. "They've given you a folder, a number. You're a project now. We used to be friends, Lace. I don't want to see you in jail."

She maneuvers around the "used to" in her head, the weighty factuality of it, the pang it gives her. A little corner of her mind compares it to the sound of her nickname from his mouth.

Alex hands her a business card. "Call me if you have any questions."

"It was good of you to let me know," she says.

• • •

Lacey thinks through it on the bus home. Behind her, two dozen of her high school students are huddled up against each other, talking and laughing and sleeping on each other's shoulders. These are the coziest memories of her own time in robotics marching band a decade ago, sharing a seat with

Alex, watching old Drum Corps videos they'd saved on their tablets, trying to come up with new ideas, or just giggling at ridiculous old jokes, gleeful and easily amused with exhaustion.

Lacey's always known this was going to happen. She didn't think she'd hear it from Alex himself, but she knew. JM has tech, and JM has plenty of connections with the cops, in Illinois and all over, and JM has a small army of lawyers. That's why her notes and drawings are all in neatly organized paper notebooks, her files with scanned copies encrypted and secured under a fake name online, why she insists people call her if they have questions about their robots instead of emailing. But that could only get her so far.

She could slow things down for a while. Or she could leave. It's what she's always planned on doing, eventually. Edsel and Amber (and Schuyler and probably Rose and maybe Mason) know enough to help keep people's machines in order, and they're smart and eager and they get why it's important. At least, she thinks they do. They're good kids, but that's a lot to put on them. Too much.

If she leaves, Madrid will slip in JM's priorities. Maybe that's safer for everyone.

But. JM's weak at the moment. She can dig into it later— could be some expansion to the west coast has them overextended, or some investments abroad—but she should be using it. She needs to speed up, not slow down.

And that was always the fundamental difference between Alex and her, wasn't it? It was a stupid risk to steal the backup robots and reprogram and reoutfit them to do her chores on the farm in high school, and it had been an even bigger one to go to college. For Alex, going to work for JM was safe, and since his parents were still tens of thousands of dollars in debt on their combine, the employee assistance was just a bonus.

Lacey left but swore she'd come back, for Madrid, for Alex, for every problem she didn't know how to solve yet. She made friends in college, the kind she could come back to, the kind who traded ideas with her late at night and didn't back down from them in the morning, but she was always going to leave them.

It's dark outside, but the bus sways on, and Lacey can tell they're nearing Madrid because the fields aren't tagged with illuminated IP labels anymore, and solar houses with herbs and vegetables loom like strange translucent creatures on the edge of her vision. It's strange, she thinks, that the more she does, the closer she gets, the less Madrid looks like the town she grew up in, the town she missed so much.

When Lacey returned to Madrid three years after college, she came with enough equipment from her dead startup to fill two barns. By then, Alex was long gone, on the other side of a divide Lacey didn't know how to start crossing.

But Lacey wants him back, and she wants what's best for her town, and she knows that now's the time. She has to make her play.

• • •

Lacey's team has three weeks until state. Thousands of people will come to watch the winning teams perform, to mill around the JM campus and stadium, to buy from food trucks and watch seed shows. For high schoolers, there's the job fair. JM will continue their streak, snapping up the most promising candidates for their four-year training rotations and overpaid engineering jobs that leave workers trapped up in NDAs and noncompetes and too much information to be useful somehow, overselling DRM-locked equipment that only works on their seeds. Not that Lacey's biased.

She is working hard, as are her students. From 7:30 a.m to 6 p.m., the band's machines are all theirs, and Lacey takes advantage of this by adding early morning practices to after-school time. Her students show up yawning, with coffee and tea in thermoses that they pretend to feed to their machines. Marching robots are roughly composed of a box on wheels, speakers, and some combination of brightly painted limbs, but most students draw marker faces with angry eyebrows or goofy smiles on the upper box. Schuyler and Mason work on balance and flexibility on the wheels and, after hours of hard work, achieve the first robot wheelie south of I-80. With this kind of talent and dedication, Lacey thinks they can't lose.

Each kid has three robots under their control, sometimes four or five for the upperclassmen. With their machines, it's not so much a matter of precision—that's the norm—but of cohesion and flair. They got third at state last year, but Lacey is counting on winning this year. Her robots' fake wrists can turn and loop; their fingers can grab with varying degrees of pressure, and this makes them the best colour guard at state

—in any division.

Those fake wrists and dexterous fingers make them useful for moving soil blocks, too, for prodding seeds into little wells and packing soil down on top. They keep track of watering schedules as well as musical scores—better, really—and the tilling attachments that fit on the trumpet section come in handy in late spring. And that's why, when her students go home after practice every day, most of them take a machine with them, rolling alongside their bikes or pressed, compact, in the back of their cars. After they leave, Lacey puts the rest in her pickup and takes them to a few drop-off spots: the corner between Lillian Wang's greenhouses and Salem Lester's sweet corn patch, surrounded by solar fence because of the damned raccoons, the park in the town centre, the gravel lot between Tracy King's cow field and Kevin Chanhira's apricot and apple orchard.

Between 6 p.m. and 7:30 a.m., people can do whatever they want with the marching machines, as long as they've talked to Lacey first and have them charged by the end. She teaches a Saturday afternoon class on weekends they're not practicing, going over the basics of what machines are and aren't capable of, how they're fixed, what instructions they need, and how they use the information.

The other teams at state won't have been sharing machines with anyone, let alone farms, but Lacey thinks it's an advantage. Over the past four years she's been coaching the band, she's found that what's good for the plants is usually good for the band too.

Lacey's building more machines, still, with her own money and the parts from the barns. She has diagrams for dozens more. She was planning on starting to sell them at cost this summer, instructions and diagrams included. Now she'll have to get it all set up within weeks.

She doesn't know how much of a difference it'll make. Even though the JM office in Madrid has downsized, the ones a couple counties over are doing just fine. Everyone there is still growing corn and soybeans like their parents, locked in debt cycles they ignore with Midwestern stoicism.

Lacey has a JM tractor of her own in the machine shed behind the barn. It's an old model, inherited, but it can already do a lot more than plant patented corn and soybeans.

• • •

Lacey comes into morning practice a little later than usual one morning, swearing at herself for leaving her tea on the kitchen counter. That's why it takes her a minute to see the row of teenagers crossing their arms at her.

"What's happening?" she asks, immediately running through a list of emergency scenarios in her head. "What's wrong?"

"You're working too hard on this project for state," Schuyler says, handing Lacey a cup of coffee. "We're going to help."

Lacey takes a sip and grimaces at the taste. "That's very kind," she says, "but I don't know what you're talking about."

The five of them present her with their evidence. Notes she left on her desk with formation diagrams, late nights, some code she fed to a marcher and forgot to replace with the standard. Nothing strong enough to get her in trouble, but enough dots for smart kids to connect.

"If you know what this is about," she says, "you know this could be dangerous. You'll lose any chance of a job with JM. They may be able to blacklist you." She swallows. "Full disclosure, they might try to have me arrested. They might succeed."

"We'll be OK," Edsel says, poised as always. "We'll mostly focus on the exhibition. Stick to the legal stuff where we can."

Lacey fidgets. "My plan isn't perfect. It's barely even formed. Is that really worth risking your futures over?"

Amber gestures at the workroom, and she seems to encompass everything—the wind kites on the roof, the greying walls, the smallness of it all. "What futures, really? Most of us are going to stay here after we graduate and farm or raise animals. The robots are our best bet. If we don't do something, if we just keep moving along until someone stops us, we'll be back in JM's showrooms, signing away what we don't even have."

"And," Edsel adds, "I read an article about JM being in trouble with a lender because of some faulty investments they made in West Africa. Now's the best chance we've got."

"It's not fair that any of this should be on you," Lacey says.

Amber shrugs. "Life's not fair. JM's business model isn't fair. We should still try."

It seems too easy to say it like that, but maybe she's right. Lacey could use the help, and they're offering. They've been paying more attention than she realized. It's their town too. "OK," Lacey says. "You want to use the exhibition if we win?"

They all nod.

"Do you have a plan for it?"

Schuyler grins. "My understanding is that we have to make the biggest, most attention-grabbing scene we can and then throw information at them until they can't ignore it." He throws an arm around Mason. "Lemme tell you, Ms. Clemmens, Mason and I are great at making a scene."

Mason nods. "Our genuine specialty."

That's at least worth a smile. "They could find a way to wave it away," she offers, a last feeble attempt.

"Not if we make it big enough!"

"But—"

"No buts," Rose says. She's always been quiet, but she looks Lacey in the eye. "We want to help." She shrugs, knowing her point is won. "And your odds are better if we do."

"This is the most irresponsible thing I have ever done," Lacey says, and then she starts explaining how they're going to do it.

• • •

Lacey is too impulsive for her own good and too stubborn by far. Everyone's always said it. This must be why she calls Alex the Saturday morning a week before state. They're halfway through a mark-by-mark run-through, and the kids have gone inside to get water and battery packs and more jar lids, and she's working on an actuator that's been rolling its triple twist too quickly.

Lacey pauses to check the instructions, in a picture on her phone, and the picture of Alex's business card is right next to it, his number autoscanned into her contacts. She presses the linked number and hits "call" before she can lose her nerve.

"Hi, Lacey," Alex's voice sounds almost warm on the phone.

She closes her eyes. "You shouldn't know what my phone number is."

"Ah, well. What can I help you with?"

Lacey swallows. His calls—and hers, if she's being honest —are probably being recorded. "It was kind of you to talk to me when we ran into each other a few weeks ago. I wanted to return the favour."

"What?"

"Alex," Lacey says his name like an anchor, lets it sink into the silence. "Is this what you really want? To work for JM forever? Because, listen. I'm going to … keep going with this. With what we discussed." She pauses, considering. "I want you to help me. Help me with it, help me get away with it, whatever."

She hears his hissed intake of breath.

"You shouldn't have told me that."

"I trust you," she says. "I think you're better than this." It's mostly true.

"I'll see you on Saturday, Lace."

• • •

Lacey and her five students work beyond the extra hours the whole team is already putting in. She orders them pizza three nights in a row, and then, beset by guilt, brings in salads and containers of radishes, turnips, and carrots from her greenhouse, most of which are politely ignored.

Edsel and Amber are in charge of the extra robots, the ones that don't have to meet the competition specifications because they aren't for the competition. Once they finish the choreography, Schuyler and Mason work on the website, researching the environmental effects of monocultures and herbicide-resistant genetics and arguing over how they're going to format their citations. Lacey stops what she's doing sometimes to give them a monologue about the ethics of IP law, which they nod at and ignore because they already wrote that whole page and she's not telling them anything they don't already know.

Lacey grins to herself sometimes on these late nights, thinking about how much these kids care, watching them do the work. The glow of computer screens and flat overhead lighting lights up their space in the shop, and Lacey's water heater is bubbling in the background, the smell of tea and coffee mixing with motor oil. They don't talk much, hunched over their computers or their robots, but they're connected all the same.

Rose works on the pamphlet, the scan codes for the website, the graphics. She goes outside one evening and throws paper around in the wind, different shapes and sizes, different weights. Somehow this turns into a spreadsheet she and Cass are working on, weighing the benefits and drawbacks of their paper options, and then Cass is there too on the nights when she doesn't have to take care of the animals, shrugging herself around Rose like a favourite cardigan.

They leave the diagrams for Lacey to fret over. She brings parts into the shop to take pictures of on the grimy concrete floor and considers sketching them out instead. She stares at the JM logo, carefully stamped on each individual part, and thinks about how illegal it all is.

And that's the other side of the work they're doing, the fear. When she's getting in the middle of Schuyler and Mason's argument about citation styles or timing the seconds it takes two pieces of confetti to fall from equal heights for Rose, it hits her hard, like hands around her ribcage, around her throat. These kids are *kids*. She's doing the diagrams, she's directing them, she's careful that they not put anything in writing or online. They probably won't go to jail, but the black mark they're putting on their future will be all too real, and she won't be able to protect them, won't even be around.

But then again, most of them are seniors. Next year, a couple of them might head to college, but most of them are going to be in Madrid, same as ever. Lacey remembers being in high school—in this high school, in this town—all too well. She thinks she's stuck in parallels sometimes, the past, present, and hoped-for future a constant replay in her head.

But she needs to put behind the fond ghosts of the past and work in the moment for the future as she envisions it—a community growing a range of crops, working on the technology together, free of the looming shadow of corporate debt.

That's what Lacey wants for her students. Even better, they want more for themselves. They'll protect each other, she knows.

• • •

They leave for state at 5 a.m., Lacey ushering yawning students into the bus, checking that they have all their tools. They settle into seats quietly, pulling sweatshirts and blankets over themselves. Lacey is wide awake, nearly vibrating with anxiety. She checks the code on her laptop, checks her bag for oil and spare parts. She talks to the bus driver, a formality given the self-driving mechanism, and straightens the cuffs on her sweater. This kind of nervous energy usually dissipates once she's done what she needs to; today it lingers. Back at her house, her car is packed. Once they're back in Madrid she's heading east, the fastest way out of JM's stronghold. She'll stay with college friends, pick up the language of startups and cities again, keep moving.

So Lacey looks out the window and watches for the first signs of daylight washing over the sky in creeping pastels, watches the sun rise and spread long shadows over the fields. The farther they go, the more corn and soybeans she sees, identifiable by the IP labels on the fences. She starts counting telephone poles.

The nervous energy follows her all day. She takes it to setup and check-in, where they take a classroom for their machines and warm them up, but by the time it's time for them to actually perform, it's been replaced by a kind of exhausted calm. She watches her students walk up to the judges and bow, a relatively steady line of jeans and dark blue T-shirts, and clear the field. The drum-major robot starts, a particular point of pride, and creates its own stand. It bows to the judges and salutes while the rest of the robots take their positions, the colour guard rolling different flags to the front beforehand. The drum major's first finger extends into a long baton, and it starts the performance.

Lacey isn't entirely present in her body for the performance, just conscious of the press of her fingers on her palms and the pulse of the beat in her mind. Everything happens when it should, the flags slicing across the air like morning sunbeams, the music swelling at the end, the marchers' feet lined up. She surges up with the rest of the crowd when it ends, clapping and whistling before she's aware that she's adding to the din.

When they announce the scores an hour later, she's not surprised that they've won—in their tiny division—but she still cries a little. She gives the kids a few hours of freedom while she and her core students wander back to their classroom and start to set up for the exhibition.

• • •

Alex strolls by an hour in, his green and yellow shirt practically glowing. He congratulates the kids and mentions that if they haven't checked out the career opportunities in the JM showroom, he's sure they'll still be open after the exhibition, for the winners. He mentions he met one of their teammates, a nice young man named Bruin, but hasn't seen anyone else from Madrid.

"Thanks, sir," Amber says, her brown eyes boring into him like the lasers Lacey has always dreamed of installing on her bots, "but we're not interested."

Lacey tenses. Alex pauses, resting his weight on one foot, threading his thumbs into the pockets of his jeans, and takes in what he's seeing. Lacey and six of her students looking frazzled and working hard on robot arms, angling their screens away from him, hours before the exhibition.

"All right," he says. "Good luck to you. Looks like we're going to have our biggest crowd yet."

It's that pose. The lean, the polite conversational deflection. Lacey looks at him and for a moment she's fifteen, and she finally has a friend, and he's funny and doesn't break Kit Kats before eating them. And she's eighteen, and he's moving to Peoria to start his job, and she hugged him before, but now his parents are there, so he extends a hand and tells her to take care of herself. And she's twenty at a New Year's Eve party, finally home for a break, and so excited to see Alex that she tells him everything at once—what JM's doing, the stuff she's learning about, all the ways she wants to try to fix it—and he smiles at her, too polite, and says something about the weather.

Lacey's not going to lose the battle and the war. She

wants her friend back.

Alex texts her a few minutes later, *Don't do this.*
*You could come with me.*

• • •

The exhibition show starts at eight, and as the winners of the
smallest division, they go first. Lacey watches the stadium fill,
sections full of people in green and yellow baseball caps,
sections of farmers taking an evening off to come see the
future of agricultural technology and talent.

At 8:07, the stadium lights dim, and field lights flood the
pitch. Lacey watches as Schuyler and Rose move from
teammate to teammate slowly, unobtrusively, somehow
missing Bruin. They're explaining the new plan for the
exhibition.

The drum major enters, sets its stand, bows and salutes.
The colour guard flags are red, but some of the other
machines have flags too, in yellow and green. As the drum
major starts the piece, the marchers with yellow and green
flags move smoothly into position, forming the letters J and
M. The crowd cheers.

The colour guard, red flags waving, move into a tight
circle around the JM, then in a diagonal line across it. They
begin to slowly rotate around the circle, each marcher raising
its red flag to connect in the diagonal as it reaches the crucial
point. The music swells; the crowd goes silent. Everyone is
leaning in, looking at the field, taking pictures, mouths
gaping.

Lacey releases a small marcher next to her in the stands

and watches it roll through the crowds and hop up the stairs on plastic feet. From where they're sitting below, Edsel and Amber and Schuyler will be doing the same. She knows where they're headed, to four different corners of the stadium, and she waits for a moment, enough to take one long breath. When the music swells again—there—she anticipates before she sees the confetti in the air.

The audience doesn't know whether to clap, but people do grab at the pieces of paper, waterproof, 80lb, and square because that's what Rose decided. Lacey watches as people frown at the words and the scan code, as they pull out their phones. Some of them take pictures of the diagrams on the back, instructions for a basic field model to be constructed out of parts removable from a locked JM machine.

Lacey's about to be in a lot of trouble.

But in this moment, she has anonymity. She's just another person in the stands watching the remains of a monumental mistake. She watches Amber hug Mason as Edsel pumps his fists. They're giddy with it, what feels like victory. Fear trickles down her throat into her chest. She thinks they're safe, but she can't be sure.

There's an audible hum rising through the crowd now that the music has stopped—of excitement and interest, she hopes. She hopes and hopes that the people in the stands want to look at fields and see opportunity and bright colours in a variety of crops. In the box across the stadium, JM executives are gesturing. One of them is scratching his head. Most of the others are pulling out their phones, gesturing angrily at each other. In this, and in the hum of interest, Lacey snatches at victory.

Lacey's notebooks have been disseminated. Edsel and Amber know almost everything anyway, and they know how to get in contact with her if necessary. JM can't destroy everything. A smile pulls at the side of her face, and she lets it unroll into a grin.

To her right, Alex is walking toward her, gently moving people out of his way. He could be coming to let her slip out of his fingers or to run away with her. He could be coming to detain her. She thinks she can hear his footsteps alone amid the din. Perhaps it's just her heartbeat.

She doesn't quite want to look at his face. She finds she can't bear it, at the end, to know whose side he's on.

# ABOUT THE AUTHOR

AnaMaria Curtis is from the part of Illinois that is very much not Chicago. She's the winner of the LeVar Burton Origins & Encounters Writing Contest and the 2019 Dell Magazines Award. In her free time, AnaMaria enjoys starting fights about 19th century British literature and getting distracted by dogs. You can get in touch or find more of her work at anamariacurtis.com or on Twitter at @AnaMCurtis.

# THE LONG NIGHT

## Gary Priest

I'M alone now, except for Mother's whispered reassurances that this is what's best for us all.

The long night brings with it many memories: the sunlit park, the clouds bullied from the sky, leaving nothing but uncluttered blue and my true love.

"I'm leaving you." She sat next to me on a park bench in a yellow dress. Her hair golden, mouth a quizzical shifting horizon unable to decide how sad to be at the words she had just spoken.

Looking out at the grey winter blanket above, it is hard to imagine how a sky could ever have been so blue as it was on that day. The greens are gone forever, the greys in charge, and the long night is everything.

"We don't belong together," I said, my tongue too thick

as I spoke the oft-repeated farewell.

"The spirit of summer and the dead of winter. Not exactly happy-ending material." Her eyes were misted, but her voice clear and fluid. How it cracked and warped and wept as Autumn took her hand and led Summer away later that day.

Autumn, a cool loner, aloof and understated, sat beside me when he returned. "Some rules don't change," he said, voice a gravel pit, eyes ringed with black. "No matter how much they fuck her up, Mother decides when Summer leaves."

The park still buzzed with children and parents orphaned from reality on their phones.

"Look at them. They don't care that she's gone, as long as the sun still blazes, and they can top up their tans, and abandon their offspring to its warm kindergarten. It doesn't matter that the true Summer no longer kisses their cheek. It's their neglect of our Mother that keeps them warm when they should be feeling your chilly breath."

Autumn sighed. "At least I still get to skin all the trees alive, eventually." We laughed, possessed, as we were, by the same sense of humour born of these shortening days and lengthening nights.

I miss Autumn. He was not one for long conversations, but his gloomy outlook matched mine, and he was my link to her.

Created to come and go long before me by our benevolent Mother, Summer was long kept apart from me. Our first meeting, many thousands of years ago, was an anomaly, a quirk of the Mother, not some later perversion of humanity.

I woke, bewildered, lost, and out of season. Summer sat naked in a field of grass. Naked was the norm then. "Oh, hello," she said, as she squinted at me in the rays of the glory that was the midday sun. I sat up, hand on my cheek, the heat alien on my skin.

"What ... is this?"

She smiled. "Grass, bugs, blue skies, and sunlight. Wonderful isn't it?"

"No. It's ... wrong. Where is the grey? Why does my skin sting with this feeling?"

"It's warmth. Haven't you ever felt it before?"

I shook my head and stood. My legs were weak. I was suddenly aware of the concept of nudity as her smile widened. I was naked and so was she. We looked at each other.

"You come from a cold place." Her giggle added gleeful punctuation to her words.

• • •

It's always dark now. The memory is colder than the shadows on this December night, a few days before Christmas.

When the end came, I settled in the southeast of a small island. There is just me and Mother left. She is distant, stern, and yet still loving.

After my first encounter with Summer, our meetings became more frequent. I was around for a few days in July one year, I spent a week in May with Spring waiting for her while killing lambs and daffodils with a sharp frost. It was not my cold heart, nor Mother's will. It was the damn mouth breathers.

They loved their cities, inventions, and so-called progress so much that they never once saw Mother's disapproving frown, or if they did, they just ignored it, denied it, and carried on.

Before the turn of the twenty-first century, Mother used to speak to her four children, but since the start of that new millennium, she had become silent. Autumn thought she was dead. I refused to believe that.

• • •

"That outfit isn't going to work in this heat," Summer said as I awoke. This time I was in the gutter and she sat on a wall opposite in white shorts and a *New Order* T-shirt. It was 1989.

I got up and sat beside her in my thick black woolen jumper and midnight-blue jeans. It was dark, but barely. Summer owned the night with her humidity and that sticky feeling that the sun never really gave up the sky at this time of year.

I pulled off my sweater. "Does it have to be this damn hot?" I asked, my mood grouchy at being pulled from my slumber for an August snowstorm.

Summer leaned in and kissed me. "Miss me?"

I pulled her close and returned her kiss. I thought I heard Mother grumble in a thunderhead in the distance, but she was never one to interfere. "How long has it been?" I asked.

"Twelve years." She put her hands around my neck as we

settled in for a smooch.

"The gaps are getting shorter," I said between kisses.

"Why doesn't Mother do something? Another ice age. A clean slate."

I couldn't help but smile at Summer suggesting an ice age, but there was no humour in my heart. "It's never been her way," I replied. "They'll be gone soon enough and she'll repair all they have spoiled."

"And we'll die."

I nodded.

I stayed too long that summer of '89. Right up until the Reading Festival. The year it went from metal to indie and it rained like a bastard.

• • •

By Christmas 2019, the heatwave of the previous year left me sleeping until my appointed day. It was still warm enough to be haunted by Summer's lips against mine, by the smoothness of her skin made silver by the moon, but as soon as I saw Autumn sat at the foot of my bed I knew I would not be seeing her this year.

His long hair, unkempt as always, his brown eyes sorrowful and wide, he waited for me to shake off my sleep. I sat up. "December already?" I asked.

He nodded. "Heatwave. I've barely started on my tasks. A huge backlog in the buttercup cull. Man these fucking mammals are screwing with my schedule."

"How is she?"

"Exhausted." He frowned, his mouth turned down. "I've

got a message from her."

"Tell me."

"It's from her, nothing to do with me."

"OK, I understand, now will you tell me what she said?"

Autumn scratched his stubbled chin. "It's soppy."

"By the holy Mother, just tell me!"

Autumn spoke Summer's words. "My love, this heat is not the tenderness that Mother first bestowed on me. It's a shrill thing, a brittle attack of Celsius. I miss the coolness of your skin and the chill of your lips. I fear our days together may be ending. I fear my heart will soon be empty of everything but this murderous heat." Autumn coughed and made a hurried exit.

Those early days of the twenty-first century seem so long ago now. I have not seen my love for centuries. The mouth breathers are all gone, swallowed in the vengeful fever of her hollow heart. It seems that Mother was not so reluctant to act after all.

All it took was a manufactured meet-cute and the willful ignorance of humanity to create a doomed romance where we saw less and less of each other and, in the end, a brokenhearted Summer erased Mother's enemies from the earth. I was angry when I realized how Mother had used us to wipe out humanity, but now I see it is for the best.

When my lover expended all her sadness, mine followed. The planet is now blanketed in ice and darkness. I will protect it until Mother has repaired and recast it once more. The blank slate where life will flourish anew, hopefully in a wiser, more respectful form than what went before.

For new children to be born the old ones must die.

I am the last of the first. Spring, Autumn, and my beloved Summer all are dead, to be reborn once Mother has reclaimed all that was taken from her. On that first day, the long night will be over, and I will find my rest, and I hope the warm embrace of my true love.

## ABOUT THE AUTHOR

Gary Priest writes short fiction and poetry. He has over thirty publications online and in print including *Daily Science Fiction*, *The Eunoia Review* and *Literary Orphans*. He lives in the UK at the end of a dead-end road, which may explain everything.

# SEA TURTLES

## Monica Joyce Evans

I don't know how it happened, only one day he was my son
and the next he wasn't. It's been a month, and now he's a sea
turtle.

He never even liked sea turtles. I don't remember them
from his childhood, sea turtles or llamas or little grey owls, all
those pastel animals that end up in cribs and bed sheets,
behind pillows. The fluffy places that he grew out of.

We sent him to college and two months later they sent
him back. Slow, they said, and sluggish. We heard the terms
"deferred scholarship" and "nonacademic withdrawal" and
"student Access-Ability," which is a pun we think. It all
meant: he's not what we thought when we accepted him.
Send him back if he changes for the better.

And now he's a sea turtle. Who doesn't need a bachelor's
degree in public policy, that's for sure.

Apparently, he volunteered.

He explained it to me once in high school. Sea turtles were going extinct, he said. I know, I told him over sliced oranges and a banana, probably there was cereal too. I know they're going extinct. They've been going extinct since I was a little girl, and that was a long time ago.

I know, Mom, he said, but now it's really happening. Now we have to do something to save them.

Why, I remember asking, pouring coffee into a mug. He'd started drinking coffee, about the same time he grew the thin mustache he wouldn't shave. Maybe his father could talk to him about the mustache, I thought, handing him the mug and meeting his eyes, and that might have been the moment when he decided. Maybe. Because he looked at me like I was an alien thing, with revulsion that I could question the worth of sea turtles.

I mean, I said—floundering at this large, male creature that was my son, that had been such a small bundle years ago —I mean, isn't it sort of a natural thing? Not that it's a good thing, but it happens, you know.

Nothing is natural anymore, he said.

The last time I saw my son, before he was a sea turtle, I don't remember what I said to him. I feel like I should. We'd had a nice day, a nice lunch, just a boy and his mother, somewhere close to a college campus. A different college, one we thought he should consider, maybe. Closer to home. I had an errand to run, new sheets or something, and we took some time out of his day to catch up. He'd become guarded by then. Friendly, warm enough, but everything we talked about was surface water, smooth and shining. Nothing beneath the surface, not that he would let me see.

I mean, I had no idea anything was wrong. I thought that things were getting better.

And I don't remember the last thing I said to him. It was probably goodbye, or I love you, or I'll see you soon.

I hope it was I love you.

Sea turtles, I've learned since, are not good mothers. None of them. There were seven kinds, and now there are four, and they all have names like leatherback and hatchback and green beak something. They lay their eggs in the sand, and when it's warmer, more of them hatch as girls. "And that's the problem," my son had told me, maybe on that last day. "There's nothing but girls out there now. One generation, and then no more sea turtles." And he stabbed at his lunch like it made him angry.

There's nothing anybody could have done, though, I said. I mean, you can't just make the sea colder.

"Can't we?" he said. He was so angry about big things, global things. Not things that should have mattered to him. He should have been a kid still, I thought, worried about classes and girls, or boys. I think I changed the subject.

But we were never anything but supportive of his choices. Even when he left school, even when he made friends we didn't like, all these bright-eyed, intense people. Even when he took medication, or didn't take medication. He was my son. What else was I supposed to do?

The last time I saw him, he gave no warning at all.

I go down to the beaches now. More often than you might think. The weather is nice sometimes, and the sand feels good on my toes. There are no sea turtles near where we live, and I don't think there ever will be again. But I get pictures from him sometimes. When they set him up— stripped him truly naked, nothing more than a brain and a stem, and put his body away, and stuck him in that big male turtle—when they did that, they gave him all sorts of things, tracking devices. Cameras. He doesn't text, but he sends me pictures when he can.

I don't understand them. They're just blue, or maybe green, and wavy. Sometimes with bits that might be plastic, might be something else. Most don't look like anything at all. I suppose he's out there fertilizing eggs, making more sea turtles, and it's not the same as getting married, but he's my son.

Anyway, I spend a lot of time at the beach. Looking out into the waves, wondering if he's ever come up on these shores. Wondering what kind of life my son has now, who can't call home but sends pictures of blue water and plastic and undersea concerns. I look at them, the pictures, the images, standing there barefoot on the beach, and when it gets too dark to see, I go home.

# ABOUT THE AUTHOR

Monica Joyce Evans is a digital game designer and researcher who also writes speculative fiction. Her short fiction has appeared in multiple publications including *Analog*, *Nature: Futures*, and *DreamForge*. She lives in North Texas with her husband, two daughters, and approximately ten million books. You can reach her at monicajoyceevans@gmail.com.

# BENEATH EVERYTHING THE FUTURE STILL EXISTS

## Maggie Chirdo

WE, pedestrians, gaze with morbid fascination at the ripped-open
    streets,
sewers and catacombs exposed,
burst pipes and city sinews stitched back together.
A place like this was
built on mass casualties.

Each day we walk right above thousands,
their fingertips scratching towards the soles of our shoes.

Kobayashi Issa wrote:

*In this world*
*we walk on the roof of hell,*
*gazing at flowers.*

The roof party is bound to end at some point
and we'll descend as well.
Maybe not to hell, but
unlikely to ever be unearthed.

Yesterday i made rice and black beans for dinner,
added spices,
sat by the window to finish a book.
I'm anyone, stretching back hundreds of years.

We, echoes,
buy flowers for ghosts
the last people with big dreams.
No matter where they rest
they reach up—remind us who we are,
they shout:

THE FUTURE STILL EXISTS
AND YOU ARE TIME-TRAVELLING

DON'T LET ANYONE TELL YOU
THIS IS THE BORING ROUTE

THE FUTURE IS A PRIVILEGE
THE FUTURE IS NOT GONE YET!

# ABOUT THE AUTHOR

Maggie Chirdo writes about American history, LGBTQ communities, pop culture, books, fashion, and whatever else keeps her up at night. Her poetry and journalism can be found in *The Interlude*, *Entropy Magazine*, *Bitch*, *Texas Observer*, and at maggiechirdo.com. She loves cable-knit sweaters and still believes in the future.

# YARD WORK

## Kevin Lauderdale

CARLOTTA said, "The first rule of yard work is—"

I held up my hand to stop her. "Hold on," I said. "I saw this in a movie. Let me guess. The first rule of yard work is: 'You do not talk about yard work.'"

Life is a movie. Sometimes it's *Fight Club*.

Carlotta shook her head.

OK, sometimes it's not *Fight Club*, even if you actually are in Los Angeles.

We were standing in front of that day's client. Or rather, that night's. They had told me when I started that sometimes it would be daytime and sometimes it would be nighttime. Depended on what the Department wanted. This job, my first, just happened to be a night one.

We were in Northridge. Just off Reseda, not quite at Cal State. We'd driven past all the blocky apartments into where the single-family houses were.

Our white Department truck was parked in front of a classic single-story ranch house: beige stucco exterior, grey wood-shake roof. Double front door, double windows next to that, and an attached garage. It looked a lot like my dentist's office, actually.

The lawn was perfect.

It was one-thirty in the morning. There was only a crescent moon, and the streetlamp was at the other end of the block, but I could still see that the lawn was lush and green. So green. Even in the dark, you could tell. We were in the third year of what everyone was now calling the Great Drought, and an awful lot of water had gone into keeping that lawn so ... verdant. And it had been edged like someone had crawled around it with nail scissors.

The musky sweet smell of jasmine hit me. There were plenty of the white, star-shaped plants on either side of the house, and the hot Santa Ana winds blowing all the way from the desert stirred them. Back when I had been a kid growing up here, the Santa Anas were pleasantly warm. Now they were just plain hot. Even in December.

As with any strong wind in L.A., it made me look up. There was a skinny palm tree on the lawn, about a foot away from the sidewalk. Its trunk raced up fifty or sixty feet. When it gets windy, sometimes palm fronds are knocked loose and fall. They can be as big as a dog, and some have sword-sharp points. A guy could get run through.

Life is a movie. Sometimes it's *Jason and the Argonauts* (Seven skeleton fighters; seven swords.

#RayHarryhausenForever).

I heard the fronds rustling and crackling above me. Was it the wind or the rats some people said nested at the tops of palms? I took a step back, placing myself out of the way in either case.

Carlotta reached in through the truck's rolled-down front-seat window and pulled out her hard hat. I'd been wearing mine ever since we'd left the dispatch office. No Dayglo orange. They were black. Of course. What else would you wear for a night job? I felt cool and stealthy in it. Plus they went great with our blue denim uniforms. Of course, I'd had to roll up my sleeves, and neither of us was wearing an undershirt. Too hot even at night.

Carlotta spoke quietly and slowly. "The first rule of yard work is: 'It's never personal.'"

I nodded. "It's—"

"Shhh. It's the middle of the night. Quietly."

"'It's never personal.'" I said in hushed tones. "Got it."

"You better Got It, kid. It's all about the Department. What they want goes. Sometimes the homeowner might try to talk to you. A good-looking young guy like you, maybe the lady of the house invites you in. Maybe the man of the house even. Some of the bigger places, maybe the maid or the butler. They want to do something extra for you, so you'll do something extra for them." She held up a finger that declared as assuredly as any burning bush: I AM THE LORD THY GOD WHEN IT COMES TO YARD WORK. "Do not."

Life is a movie. Sometimes it's *The Ten Commandments*.

Carlotta took a deep breath and continued in an almost-whisper, "You are working for the Department. You are an employee of the Los Angeles Department of Water and Power. You do not get personal. You are not here because you want to be. You are not here for any reason of your own. You are not here because you like—"

"Or dislike," I added.

"*Exactamente*. Glad you paid attention at orientation. Or *dislike* anyone personally. You are here to work."

"I am here for the Department," I said, throwing a noble and dramatic spin on it. "I act out their will. Ooo! Like I'm an actor and the Department is my director."

"Shh! Yeah. Sure. Whatever."

I nodded. I wanted to make a good impression. Carlotta was two or three times my age, and she clearly knew her stuff. Someone had told me she'd been with the DWP since the Nineties. I was honoured she'd taken me on.

I'd been out of college for six months, which meant my student loan repayments had just kicked in. You'd figure in Los Angeles there would be a lot of positions for someone with a B.A. in history and a minor in film studies. I'd always figured I could get a job in the movies, checking things to make sure no anachronisms crept in. No kilts in *Braveheart* because no one would wear them for a couple more centuries. No Raquel Welch poster in *The Shawshank Redemption* because *One Million Years B.C.* didn't come out until the year after Andy escaped. Then there's that kid wearing a digital watch during the Civil War in *Glory* ...

Hollywood needed people like me to check things like that. Or so I'd thought. Turns out, even in Hollywood, you can't really make up your own job. There was nothing in the *Times* or on Craigslist about a professional anti-anachronism checker. There weren't even any mail room jobs for me to start in and work my way up. There weren't any mail rooms anymore. It was all email.

Time was, somebody in my position might go get a job with the post office. But the USPS wasn't hiring either. Budget cutbacks. So ... the LADWP. It's one job they can't outsource to India or Mexico. The snowpack up in the Eastern Sierra Nevada, the aqueducts, the powerhouses, and the wires are all right here and they aren't going anywhere. So the pay's not great, and the hours suck, but ...

Life is a movie. Sometimes it's *The Wizard of Oz*. And, as Frank Morgan as the Wizard says: "Times being what they were, I accepted the job."

"The second rule of yard work is: 'Always check your paperwork.'" From out of nowhere, it seemed, Carlotta produced a clipboard. "OK, kid, what does the sign say?"

I looked up. "Allen Street. Number Three-Four-Two."

"Excellent, kid. That's what it says here on the paper. You do not want to do your job at the wrong place. First of all, you'll only have to do it again at the right place. Plus, the place you did do it — *Ay!* They wake up in the morning and see someone's messed with their yard ... No, kid. And the Department will hear from them, you can bet. Not good for you."

She led me around to the side of the truck and opened one of the boxy compartments. The door swung up slowly on silent hinges. "Custom-made for the Department," Carlotta said. "Because rule number three of yard work: 'Be quiet.' You are not supposed to disturb the homeowner. You got that, kid? In the best-case scenario, you never interact with the homeowner at all. Believe me, they don't want to see you, so you don't want to see them."

She pulled out two pairs of gloves and handed me one. She pointed across the street.

"That guy over there replaced his whole lawn with a rock garden. That's smart. We're all supposed to be using fifty percent less water. Even less eventually. Guess that's the easy way."

Life is a movie. Sometimes it's Lynch's *Dune*. If you're lucky, it's *Lawrence of Arabia*. But it's usually Lynch's *Dune*.

I pointed to the house on the left of 342. "*That's* the easy way," I said. I'd noticed it as soon as we'd driven up. Whoever owned it had simply let the lawn die in the Drought. Hadn't even bothered to replace it with anything. Whatever remained that wasn't dirt was yellow, brown, and scraggly. I craned my neck. The house to the right had a "lawn" of ground-cover juniper that looked like a hundred downed Christmas wreaths. There were a few cacti tossed in for decoration. I frowned. Which was worse, the totally deadbeat lawn or the half-assed lawn?

"Yeah," said Carlotta. "But I like the rocks. All rocks, no water, no yard work. Of course, that puts people like you and me out of a job." She put her hands on her hips. "But Mr. Three-Four-Two here ... A lot of work to do. He's not even one of the biggies. Someone up in Bel-Air used almost twelve million gallons of water last year."

"Makes sense. You got a big mansion, you got grounds."

"Don't they know it's the Great Drought? That Bel-Air guy is the biggest residential user in the whole of California. It's like war, kid. Supposed to be that we're all in this together. At least most people have stopped hosing down their driveways. Man, that gets to me. What do they think, it's gonna make them grow?" We walked to the back of the truck, and I pushed aside the blue plastic tarp in the bed. "I only got a ten-by-fifty strip, but I'm gonna water it 'til it's a circular driveway like up in Westwood. I don't think so. *Loco*."

She pointed, and I grabbed two shovels from the back of the truck.

"What about cones?" I asked. "Do we get to put out cones?" We had a couple dozen orange cones stacked in two piles on special mounts at the front of the truck. Marking our work zone with cones would be very professional.

Carlotta shook her head. "Nighttime. What do you think? Who's gonna see? Plus we don't want to draw attention to ourselves."

I was truly disappointed. The cones would have been cool.

Life is a movie. Sometimes it's *A Christmas Story* (Just the scene where Ralphie receives the pink bunny suit).

Carlotta scanned the lawn with the practiced eye of a surveyor. She positioned herself on the sidewalk at about the lawn's midpoint. She pointed for me to stand next to her.

"Work your way up to the house. Then you turn right and work back down to the sidewalk. I'll go to my left. Start digging."

"How deep?" I asked.

"Just an inch. Leave the topsoil. If you can roll up the lawn sod in nice long strips a foot or so wide, that's best. And fastest."

"Where's all this stuff go anyway?"

"Back east, I guess. You don't have to worry about how much water you use out there." Carlotta snorted. "Or maybe it goes to that place in Bel-Air. Hey, maybe that's why he needs all that water. He's a lawn hoarder." She laughed. "I dunno. All I know is the last rule of yard work: 'When the DWP tells you not to use so much water, you better not use so much water.'"

The house's porch light came on.

"Uh oh," said Carlotta. "They're up."

"Hey, you!" a man screamed from the front window. "Get away from my lawn! Beat it! I'm gonna kill you! I'm gonna—"

"Dig faster, kid," Carlotta said, speeding up. "Dig faster!"

Yep, life is a movie. Sometimes it's *Repo Man*.

# ABOUT THE AUTHOR

Kevin Lauderdale's work has appeared in several of Pocket Books' *Star Trek* anthologies, the journal *Nature*, and a handful of genre / "new weird" anthologies. He's a frequent guest on pop culture podcasts and hosts his own, devoted to the Golden Age of Radio, "Presenting the Transcription Feature." Visit him at kevinlauderdale.livejournal.com.

# CETACEAN REPROCESSORS, INC.

## Jason P. Burnham

"CAN you understand me?" I call through my underwater translator over the gentle slap of cold, oily blue-green water.

The massive smoky-grey Bryde's whale next to the boat doesn't react. I look timidly up to the top of their open mouth, jutting from the water like a giant white arrowhead, trap collecting their assigned section of the Great Pacific Garbage Patch. Either the cipher I bought is no good or this Cetacean Reprocessors, Inc. employee/indentured servant is ignoring me.

"I say, whale, Bryde's whale, I'm here to save you from Cetacean Reprocessors," I say, hoping this revelation will elicit a response. How can I help them if they don't listen to me?

Their mouth fills with a multitude of human detritus:

plastic bags, plastic spoons, plastic straws, diapers, bottles, microplastics invisible and innumerable. Represented are every possible hydrocarbon polymer combination, chains unbreakable on the time scale of life on Earth.

If the whale hears me, they give no indication. Mouth full, they close it, take a last breath of air, and dive to the refuse deposit chamber beneath. Once full, the chamber's buoyant raft will deflate and a submersible will guide it down into a volcanic vent for rapid breakdown.

I pick up my paddles and row to the next-nearest whale, whose mouth is still filling.

"I say, whale, Bryde's whale, I'm here to save you from Cetacean Reprocessors," I repeat.

The inrush of trash halts and the whale sputters, choking on some of the garbage.

Oh shit, I've killed a whale.

I stand at the edge of the boat and pull out my radio.

"Mayday, Mayday, this is Vince Smith of the only noncommercial boat currently floating the Great Pacific Garbage Patch. We've got a Bryde's whale down."

More trash floats out of the whale's mouth and the animal rolls and sprays through its blowhole.

"We've got names, you know," crackles a voice from my translator.

I nearly fall into the water. My stumbling around generates a spray of dirty, cold water onto my black wetsuit.

"You can understand me?" I'm so grateful the cipher works. I paid so much for it.

"Of course. Nur was ignoring you. Not too fond of humans," says the whale.

"Nur?" I ask, bewildered.

"Oh, now don't go getting worked up that a whale can be named Nur." The whale gives a short huff through their blowhole. "That's not their *real* name, it's whatever your program made it into so you can understand it."

"What's Nur's whale name?" This is not the conversation I thought I was going to be having.

"Well see, that's the thing. No matter what I tell you, that translator of yours is going to tell you Nur's name is Nur. We'll just have to call that one 'lost in translation.'"

"What do I call you?" I ask.

"Name is Yui," says the whale as it holds up a flipper.

I'm not sure why I asked. "Well, Yui, any idea why Nur didn't want to chat?"

"Look, human, if you can't guess why a whale wouldn't want to speak to you, might I suggest Baleen Google to fill yourself in on our prior encounters." Yui snorts through their blow hole as they spin away from me in the water. The boat rocks vigourously and my stomach turns.

"There's a whale Google?" I ask incredulously.

"Human, what did you say your name was?"

"Vince," I say.

"Right. Vince, if you don't know anything about us, can I ask you what you've come out here to do? Let me guess, you heard about our supposed plight on social media and thought it was your duty to come save us."

A lump forms in my throat. This whale doesn't know me. "I'm—I'm here to save you from Cetacean Reprocessors." My cheeks redden. This isn't how this is supposed to go.

Yui snorts again. The cipher pipes through a laugh. I wasn't aware whales had a sense of humour.

"Vince, I'm sure you're a good human, or think you are, but we don't need any help. Check out Nur over there."

"Nur" has resurfaced and is filling their mouth again with trash.

"What about them?" I ask, blinking rapidly to hold back … to keep the ocean spray out.

"Nur's got twenty-five grand-whales. They're old as hell." *What is whale hell?*

Yui continues after a breath. "They're old, but they love this shit. They can't think of anything better than gobbling up human trash to save the ocean for their family."

I can't believe my ears. "But you and the others are being used by Cetacean Reprocessors! They're forcing you to work without adequate compensation!"

"What do you know about what's good for a Bryde's whale?"

"Uh, I mean, um …" I stammer.

"See! You have no idea. If you knew anything about us, had ever talked to a few of us before, you'd know that we're just happy humans are participating in this process. In fact, some of us think we've bamboozled *you* into finally getting *your* act together." There's that laughter snort again.

I blink, no words forming. What *am* I doing here?

"So do us a favour, Vince?" Yui, the Bryde's whale, pauses for my reply.

I bumble, trip, over my response. "Uh, yeah, yes, Yui?"

"Stop trying to do what you think is best for us, get out a net, and start cleaning some of this crap up," says Yui. They open their mouth wide, engulf trash, and dive to the underwater receptacle.

I watch Nur splash in the distance and the cipher picks up a chuckle.

I'm mad, hurt, angry. This isn't how this was supposed to go. I turn over the motor to propel myself away, but it gets stuck on a laminated cover of *Architectural Digest*'s "Trash Dump Chic" issue.

Ugh. I survey the slimy debris, lift my eyes to the distant whale disentanglement pontoon operated by Cetacean Reprocessors. They're too far away to notice my embarrassment, the humiliation of not accomplishing what I thought I was supposed to be doing here. If nobody saw me, or I guess even if they did, what's the harm in admitting I was wrong? Yui's right after all. If I want to help, I should help how I'm needed, not how I *think* I should be helping.

"Hey Nur, can you help me find a net?" I call through the translator.

I wonder if Cetacean Reprocessors needs any more human employees. These whales are doing good work.

# ABOUT THE AUTHOR

Jason P. Burnham is an infectious diseases physician and clinical researcher. He laments his existence in a timeline wherein cat allergies are incurable. He loves spending time with his wife, kids, and dog. He strives to do his small part in the collective actions necessary to ensure the things he loves have a planet that remains habitable for them.

# FARMING WITH CRANKY

## Matt Tighe

IT'S hot. It's always hot. It is cooler up at the other end of the field under the shade of the big trees, but I still prefer it down this end, in the heat. The trees are so big, so dark and mossy and quiet—it's scary. Dad says they grow like that because of the heat. He says that a long time ago it was different.

"You are doing well." He wipes sweat from his face and smiles across at me. I sway in my saddle and of course it is right then that I almost fall. I grab at the rough scales, my hands slick with sweat, and I try to sit up straight. I don't need to look back at the house to know Mum will be watching, her hands gripping the yard fence too tightly.

I've been at Dad to let me plough since I saw Mikey next door riding. He went by high on the back of their old Steg, wedged between its back plates and looking all serious, even though I knew he was side-eyeing me the whole time.

"Keep her steady." Dad is on Cranky the Anky, borrowed

from Old Johnson for the afternoon. The dopey old thing is almost blind, and happy to just plod along next to the harnessed Trice. I hold on to the reins loosely, like Dad keeps saying, but it's hard. I'm so high up.

"Old man Johnson says they used to use machines to do this," I say.

"Your lines are good." Dad's praise makes me feel pretty good. They are, too. The black earth is turned over in long furrows that fill the air with a rich, dark smell, lines that go all the way up to the huge tangle of forest that marks the end of the reclaimed land. Mikey can side-eye my lines all he wants, he won't do any straighter.

"It's better this way," Dad says.

"Because the machines made it so hot?"

"We made it hot, honey." Dad wipes his face. "Keep her steady!" he says then, a sudden edge to his voice. I try, but the Trice tosses her head up, snorting, and then gives a little buck. I shriek and scrabble at her knobbly scales.

Then Dad curses and slips down from Cranky's back. He moves so fast he is up the knotted ladder and grabbing me from my saddle before I even really register the roaring.

He slides down, ignoring the ladder, wincing as the Trice's rough hide scrapes his back. For a moment his heart thuds against my ear as he holds me to his side, and then he dumps me on the ground.

"The house! Go!"

There is another roar from the trees. The Trice snorts and tosses her head. I freeze.

"Go!" Dad shouts again, and I run.

He runs too, but not for the house.

I stumble and then Mum is there, scooping me up like I weigh nothing and ducking back through the narrow yard gate. She puts me down and we both turn, silently frantic, wishing Dad to be safe.

He is rolling right under the fence at the battery when the beast pushes from the dark green world beyond the boundary fence. It looks small because the trees are so huge, but it's really big—big enough to bust through the boundary and charge for Cranky, its horrible mouth gaping, long tail flicking like it has a mind of its own.

"Don't watch." Mum covers my eyes.

There is a humming as Dad reroutes the power to the house fence. Maxing the solar battery only gives enough juice for one big shock, but it is a *really* big one. It would have been better if Dad had gotten the extra charge through the boundary fence in time, but at least we are safe now. Cranky and the Trice are not.

I begin to pull Mum's hand away, but then I think of the Trice, how she stands so patiently when you saddle her, how sometimes she will nuzzle you as you try to harness her. And I think of Cranky, that dopey old thing, plodding along, slow and content under the hot sun. I leave Mum's hand where it is, and my tears are hot against her palm.

• • •

Old Johnson looks mad, but then he sighs and rubs his bald head.

"I'll pay the fast-track incubation fee," Dad says.

"Ah, don't worry about it." Old Johnson sighs again. "Ain't nobody's fault. And Cranky, he was about done anyways." He rubs his head again. "Your Trice?"

It's Dad's turn to sigh. "We'll manage. We always do."

"Dad," I say. I've been thinking. Thinking about the dark forest that covers most everything. Thinking about what's in there. About why. "We brought them all back."

He looks down at me, all sweaty and hot and serious, but then he smiles a little bit.

"Yes, honey. A long time ago. They were well suited to how things had gotten. You know that. You've been down to Dobsley's, seen the incubators. Seen the babies."

"I mean we brought them *all* back."

Old Johnson rubs his head again. "Was hardly anyone left as to object, back then." He sounds sour. "Can't say I understand all the decisions that got made. Used to be we were top dogs."

Dad shakes his head and a few drops of sweat fall off his grimy forehead. It's always so hot.

"It's better this way," he says.

# ABOUT THE AUTHOR

Matt Tighe lives in northern NSW Australia with his amazingly patient wife, not so patient children, Sherlock the dog, and Mycroft the cat. He is an academic in his other life. His work has appeared in *Nature Futures*, *The NoSleep Podcast*, *Daily*

*Science Fiction*, and other places. You can find his sporadic attempts at humour on twitter @MKTighewrites and other info at matttighe.weebly.com.

# DEMETER SEEKS PERSEPHONE IN THE YEAR 2210

## Priya Chand

## 1. OVERWORLD

We, the chorus, welcome you to today's stage, a patch in the rocky landscape once known as Attica.

Close your eyes and inhale the subtle sweetness of sun-warmed grass. Hear the soft rustle of dresses, giggling young women whose whispers counterpoint the chirping birds. Soon you realize there's no variation in the birdsong, and the thought startles you into opening your eyes.

Our setting is a notch between skyscrapers. It's beautiful, in the way of the well-engineered: sunlight beams in via mirrors, splashing light across the grass, which slopes gently so as to minimize echoing. To one side is a tree, which cradles a nest that holds a single bird.

And the women, comparing holograms of flowers on their phones, wondering if any might sprout in this thing humans call a "nature preserve," having forgotten that Bermuda grass is as unnatural to this continent as concrete and plastic.

One of the women is distracted. Persephone's eyes keep slipping from the pictures—"How nice," she says, to a half-dead spray of weeds as her friends swipe through the images, no one remarking upon her absentmindedness—and then her back snaps straight, eyes focused forward.

A shadow sweeps across the meadow, a half-second glitch in the sunbeam reflectors. When the light returns, Persephone is gone.

We wail, we lament, we fill the silence left when the startled bird stopped its tinny song.

Her friends continue chatting, and for the first time you wonder why they're so intent on the details of extinct flowers. For the first time you see sweat sheened on their foreheads, a drama reenacted at gunpoint, every syllable as deliberate as the geoengineers' rain bullets.

## 2. UNDERWORLD

Daughter of laughter, we sing, daughter of Demeter. Here she is, where we have found her every year since the beginning of time.

The dog(s) recognize her. "Kerberos, *down*," Persephone

says, laughing, patting her pockets for treats she didn't bring, not knowing when she would return. She presses her hand to the ground, shapes a ball, throws it into the grey-lit distance. Drooling joy from all three heads, he scampers after it.

Persephone waits until he's out of sight before turning to face the double throne behind her, blocky seats that shimmer golden. Her mouth parts, slightly, releasing the overworld's gasoline-tinged air into this breathless space.

Shadows resolve into the tall slim figure of a man as Hades—lord of underground wealth, lord of anything but death—pulls off his helmet.

"About time," Persephone says, hands on hips. "We were out there every day for a month."

Hades shrugs. "I was waiting for the earth's scent to change." He reaches up and, although the ceiling is far overhead, takes a handful of soil from Up There. "I gave up waiting." He rubs the clod between his fingers until it crumbles into nothingness. They stare at each other, every subtlety mastered—the flick of an eyelid, twitch of the lips—as only immortals can.

The silence drags on and we fill it with song.

This, always, is their first meeting. Here, dark Hades tricks Persephone into staying in the underworld, snaring her with human ritual. Zeus and Hera have the Sacred Wedding. Hades and Persephone have ... this, the marriage rites of ancient Hellas, whose name has outlived the last olive tree.

"The balance is off," Persephone says.

We sing, loudly, do not eat of the underworld, innocent

girl!

At last her shoulders soften, her pose loses its confidence. Persephone extends her hand, and in a child's voice, "I am hungry. Please."

"Of course." Hades hides a smile, plucks a pomegranate from thin air and cracks it open. Even in the ambient lighting of his realm, each seed glistens, wine-dark at the edges, tapering into milk where they nestle against each other.

Persephone takes the seeds and puts one, two, three in her mouth. Chews. Keeps chewing.

"What is it?" Hades asks, careful to sound insouciant, knowing he has won her over.

Persephone spits the seeds back into her palm. They are unmarred. She and Hades stare at each other, horrified.

## 3. OVERWORLD

Demeter is yelling.

She is in a sensible pantsuit, every stitch bespoke, the CEO of a breakfast conglomerate: forty percent of the world's supply of grain and three proprietary pollinators—two Varroa-resistant bees and an ant immune to most fungal infections. But none of these are why her voice is echoing hoarsely through the preserve.

"Where is she?" Demeter screams. "Where is Persephone?"

We croon loss and grief. We add the high notes of a mother who, for the first time, has left her child alone and regrets it, knowing her daughter will never be innocent again.

The friends huddle together. One of them is hitching her breath, trying to force tears out. You don't think she will. Whatever emotions are in the air now, fear isn't one of them, and she is not as good an actress as she thinks. But, trying her best, she blubbers, "She was stolen."

"By whom?" All of a sudden Demeter's fury is pulled into a tight point, ready to launch. "Tell me what you saw—"

"Mother," Persephone says. By the flattening of the grass nearby, you know Hades is also present.

We stop singing.

Demeter's eyes go round and her jaw tightens. Counterfeit anger whooshes from her body. Her blazer clings to limp arms. The friends, too, have let their phones fall among the grass, backs stiff, all trace of playfulness—pretend or otherwise—gone. The one who was trying to cry is now trembling with the effort of holding in a wail.

"You're not supposed to be here," Demeter whispers.

"I know." Persephone shakes her head. "It didn't work. I couldn't eat the seeds."

"Last year you had no problem eating three."

"I vomited two!"

"Still." Demeter's head shakes. She has retreated to the role she holds in every story, the eternal mother, hiding her trembling hands in too-small pockets. "You must, my dear. Try again."

Winter, we whisper. Demeter's grief brings winter, one month for every seed Persephone eats.

"You think I didn't?" Nervous energy radiates outward

from Persephone. "Mother, I tried. I promise"—she looks at the space next to her—"Tell her, Pluton."

Hades' voice echoes, and you're not sure if it's the helmet or his presence. "We tried, Demeter. It is worse here than it was before. The soil is … different. It no longer smells of the seasons."

Demeter sits on the ground, which immediately tries to soak her clothes green. "Then we will not have winter this year." She runs fingers through the grass. A few stalks mutate, feebly, into something taller with frayed ends, something recognizable to the ancients who named her. She pulls one stem from the earth and chews on its slender length. "We will try again," she says. "We must keep trying." She frowns. "Our scientists keep adding vitamins to the food. They say it is not as healthy as it used to be. They are right. Winter brings sleep, rest. Without rest, there is no renewal."

They are so close, you can see their shadowed eyes, the tired limbs. You want to reach out and tell them. But you cannot. You make them what they are, you and every other child of the Anthropocene, and you cannot unmake what they have become. You are the setting, not the chorus.

We are listening, but we, too, need time. We were made to sing, not write new songs.

Persephone and the others are nodding to Demeter's words. Hades' helmet clanks; the friends, poor nameless nymphs, committed to their bit roles, are ready to have the same inane conversations and cower for however long it takes to bring winter back.

"Good. I will see you tomorrow." Demeter spits out the stem. It takes root and straightens up, swelling into ripeness.

There is no place for its seed to go, yet.

# ABOUT THE AUTHOR

Priya Chand grew up in San Diego and now resides in the vicinity of Chicago. She has previously been published in *Clarkesworld*, *Nature Futures*, and *Analog SF*, among others. Her interest in ecosystems stems from a background in biology and a love of marine life. When she's not reading, writing, or eating, she enjoys swimming, martial arts, and naps.

# HELIANTHUS

## Liam Hogan

"FUNNY, a vampire with SAD," I quip.

The tall Ukrainian peers through mirrored goggles. "Intolerance to sunlight does not qualify me as vampire." Leonid is our grower. It doesn't matter how clever the plant biologists are, myself newly included, if you don't have someone with green fingers to nurture your gene-hack creations. And Leonid is, everyone says, the greenest of the green.

"And SAD?"

He pauses, secateurs in hand. His own pair, never lent, scrupulously cleaned and sharpened. "Is not funny." He glances at my sandals, feet and ankles lobster red. "Being underground is no hardship, for me. Grow lamps are gentler than sun."

The first hack we do knocks out a plant's defences against direct sunlight, as well as their diurnal response. They don't need them and grow ten times faster in the vast subterranean hydroponic fields, where artificial lights always shine benignly, powered by another equally vast field far above our heads: solar panels spanning the arid desert landscape .

"Grow lamps have plenty of blue, and vitamin D supplements help." He shrugs. I'm only half listening, wondering when it will be cool enough to escape up top again. "As does regular sleep, avoid alcohol, see best in others."

I ignore the barb, if barb it was. "And these?" I gesture to the leggy yellow flowers he grows in this small corner of the complex. If he wasn't so damned talented, would we indulge him?

"These?" Sunflowers reflect in twin lenses, a constellation of otherworldly stars. "These I grow for my *soul*."

# ABOUT THE AUTHOR

Liam Hogan is an award winning short story writer, with stories in *Best of British Science Fiction 2016* & *2019*, and *Best of British Fantasy 2018* (NewCon Press). He's been published by *Analog*, *Daily Science Fiction*, and *Flame Tree Press*, among others. He helps host Liars' League London, volunteers at the creative writing charity Ministry of Stories, and lives and avoids work in London. More details at happyendingnotguaranteed.blogspot.co.uk.

# WHAT I DO TO THE EARTH I DO TO ME

## John Paul Caponigro

I find something hidden in the dirt.
I find something in me.

I sow a seed in fertile ground.
I sow a seed in me.

I grow an unfolding garden.
I grow a garden in me.

I tend a wild flock.
I tend wild me.

I bring violence to nature.
I violate me.

I poison clean water.
I poison me.

I dam a running river.
I dam me.

I flood a welcoming valley.
I drown me.

I burn a sheltering forest.
I burn me.

I smoke clear sky.
I blind and choke me.

I raze raw wastelands.
I raise wastelands in me.

I unleash a metastasizing city.
I leash wilderness in me.

I take power from this sphere.
I disempower me.

I turn terrain into a thing for myself.
I turn myself into a thing for someone else.

I grieve for our turning globe.
I grieve for me.

I heal the wonders of our world.
I heal me.

I bring forth blossoms in groves.
I bring forth blooms in me.

I savour the fruits of fields.
I savour the fruits of me.

I enrich soil.
I enrich me.

I give me back to our land.
I give me back to me.

I love our earth.
I love me.

# ABOUT THE AUTHOR

John Paul Caponigro is an internationally collected visual artist and published author. He leads unique adventures in the wildest places on Earth to help participants creatively make deeper connections with nature and themselves. View his TEDx and Google talks at www.johnpaulcaponigro.art.

# ABOUT THE EDITOR

KATRINA Archer is the author of dark fantasy *The Tree of Souls* and YA fantasy *Untalented*, a *Library Journal* Indie Ebook Award Honorable Mention. A former software engineer, she has worked in aerospace, video games, and film, and is a freelance copy editor and publisher of climate change site *Little Blue Marble*. She can operate almost any vehicle that can't fly, doesn't believe in life without books or chocolate, and together with her spouse, puts up with the antics of a sweet potato and a chaos goblin masquerading as cats. Connect with her online at www.katrinaarcher.com.

For more great fiction and features about our changing climate, join us at

*LittleBlueMarble.ca*

**Also available from** *Little Blue Marble:*

*Little Blue Marble 2021: Tipping Points*

*Little Blue Marble 2020: Greener Futures*

*Little Blue Marble 2019: Climate in Crisis*

*Little Blue Marble 2018: More Stories of Our Changing Climate*

*Little Blue Marble 2017: Stories of Our Changing Climate*

# YOU MIGHT ALSO LIKE

*Weird Fishes*
by Rae Mariz
from Stelliform Press

In this mind and heart-bending work of Hawaiian
Indigenous Futurism, a sentient squid and a sealfolk
mermaid navigate the dangers of cultural
misunderstanding in the murky waters of a climate
changed ocean. Publishers Weekly called this book
"entirely fresh and inventive" in their starred review.